IN THE NAME OF KARINA

KEN ALLEN

ISBN-13: 9798420332382
ISBN-10: 8420332382

Cover design by: Art Painter
Library of Congress Control Number: 2018675309
Printed in the United States of America

I would greatly like to thank my sister Barbara, for each time that I write a piece, hers is the first door that I knock on for feedback. I would also like to thank Brian Thompson for going through my original manuscript and Nick, a detective sergeant of the Humberside police who read it through for me to get a police perspective of it. Also many thanks to Daniel Cooper who put a lot of time and effort into helping bring the book to publication. Lastly I would like to thank Trish, my wife. She hounded me for a long time to get it published. Thanks Trish.

LOOKING BACK

"Wash the pots, then get back up to your room."

Jack didn't look across to his stepfather. He had learnt not to as it only infuriated him more. As with most nights he walked over to the sink, filled it with warm water and squeezed in the washing up liquid, careful not to put too much in as he knew without checking that Billy would be watching; any excuse to give Jack a slap. First He washed the plates before putting in the pans, and after drying everything put them carefully away.

His mother came across to Jack telling him that she would clean the sink and best go up to his room while his stepfather was in the lounge. Jack saw the half smile on his mother's face and somehow knew she loved him really. He would never know she felt powerless to stop her husband from mis-treating him and was fearful to stand up to him. Jack was only six years old. He could not recall it being any different. His sister, twelve years older than Jack had moved out to live with friends a year earlier. Jack never knew it was her way of escaping her stepfather.

On the way up the stairs he heard his stepfather.

"Has it gone up to its room?"

"Billy please don't talk about Jack like that" replied his mother.

"Shut up you silly cow."

Jack sat on his bed and cried, something he did a lot. He looked down at the bruise on the side of his lower leg. Just for not being fast enough to get out of his way. He cried again. When the mist from his eyes had cleared, he rolled up his shirt sleeve to examine the Chinese burn mark that Stuart, Billy's nine year old son had done.

The months passed by and turned into years, the mistreatment continued the same throughout. Jack, to try to feel better inside, had managed, when alone in his bedroom, to somehow detach himself and think deeply on nice things, blocking the physical and emotional abuse from his mind.

His mother had spoken to him on several occasions when she had passed his bedroom, hearing him in conversation with himself, mostly with differing voices. Each time Jack would give his mother a strange look, totally unaware of what she was talking about. He felt inadequate, insecure, and behaved strangely. At eight he had no idea it was a direct consequence of his stepfather's treatment towards him. He'd shut his bedroom door, and then pull the handle to make certain the latch had connected. When he realised that it had, he took three paces into his room but then went back once more to re-check the handle had latched. Three paces away again and back once more to re-check. This was repeated five times each time Jack entered his bedroom. When he went down the stairs (after making sure that no one was watching), on stepping from the last stair, he took three steps back up before he came back down into the hallway. He repeated this twice each time. Everything had to be formally and correctly maneuvered. If it wasn't there would be a price to pay.

By the time Jack was eleven years old

his obsessive compulsive disorder had worsened to such a degree that his mother took him to the doctors, his stepfather laughing at him had found a new source of emotionally hurting Jack.

His doctor in turn referred Jack to a psychiatrist, especially after his mother had mentioned that he talked to himself in different dialects, which Jack always denied, either being completely oblivious to, or too embarrassed to admit to; his mother never knew.

After several sessions the psychiatrist realised that Jack was telling the truth about not being aware of the conversations that took place within his bedroom that his mother heard on a regular basis. He asked Jack's mother what his home life was like, and carefully wording his questions asked if there might be any reason that Jack could possibly feel traumatised.

Inwardly panicking she said "Jack has a good home life with loving parents. Perhaps we should bring the sessions to an end," suggested his mother, frightened of any repercussions from her husband.

"I strongly advise them to continue for Jack's sake. The only reason that I asked the question is that I strongly believe that Jack has developed dissociative identity disorder, and on occasion that can be attributed to early trauma within a child's life, but not every time. I would advise continued treatment and assessment".

"Jack has never been traumatised in any way."

"I'm sure that's the case, but it is of the upmost importance that Jack continues with the sessions as we need to know the full extent of his mental health to be able to offer the correct course of treatment for Jack's well being."

His mother asked what dissociative identity disorder was, with the psychiatrist explaining that it was more commonly known as multiple personality disorder and without the correct treatment could get worse. After arranging a further appointment she took Jack home, constantly looking at him, weighed down with guilt and angry with herself for not stepping in to protect her son over the years; determined to do so from now on.

Over the following year Jack's mother regularly went into her own bedroom when Jack was in his room so that she could hear any conversation that was taking place. She felt that she needed to monitor Jack's progress for his own sake, and to pass the information on to the psychiatrist, who had told her to be very careful as if Jack found out it could hinder his recovery and destroy his trust in the only place he felt safe in within his own mind. He also warned her not to confront Jack on anything he said within his own bedroom.

After his mothers intervention, his stepfather softened his ways with Jack, now thirteen, but not completely, and there was virtually no conversation between Jack and his stepfather, but unfortunately Stuart, now sixteen stepped up his bullying. Each week he made Jack give him half of his pocket money, an arrangement secured by hitting Jack regularly on the first three weeks of refusal.

Stuart had started buying and smoking cannabis, and it wasn't long before he had introduced Jack to it, as a way of extracting more money from him.

To Jack the cannabis was a Godsend, releasing the torment of his bullying. It was a welcome relief but not long before reality returned.

Over time, after hearing Jack talking in five different voices in his bedroom, his mother informed the psychiatrist and more appointments were arranged to re-assess him.

Several weeks later, Jack in by himself, his mother arrived back home to find his cats bloody body laid out on the front doorstep, next to a brick, with blood on it. She shouted for Jack to come down from his room.

"Have you seen the cat?"

Jack shrugged his shoulders and started back up the stairs.

"You come back down here now. What happened to the cat? It's dead."

Jack only shrugged his shoulders again, a non-caring look upon his face.

"Oh my God. Jack you've killed him haven't you?" his mother asked, trembling. It was the first time she saw the cold stare on Jacks face.

"You speak to me now" demanded his mother loudly.

His stare slightly softened. "I'm sorry mam. A voice in my head told me I had to do it." He never said another word; only looked longingly into his mother's eyes, expecting her forgiveness.

"Have you done anything like this before?'" she questioned frighteningly.

"No. I promise you." he replied. "I have been trying to ignore the voice in my head."

"Jack you must promise me that you will never do anything like this ever again, and if you hear the voice again, you must tell me immediately."

Jack nodded and went up to his room, watched all the way by his mother, her hand across her mouth, fear in her eyes.

She decided against telling the psychiatrist, as frightening as it was, hoping it was just a one off, being fearful of any repercussions by the authorities if they knew about Jack's state of mind.

As the sessions of therapy continued, Jack's mothers health declined rapidly.

At fifteen I started buying my own cannabis and smoked myself regularly into oblivion, wishing I had a gun to blow all four of us away; to finish my worthless life and to release mum from her prison.

She died in my arms after a heart attack, her last word to me. "Sorry". Seeing the sadness in her eyes would remain with me forever.

I thought constantly about the stress they both put my mother under. I was inconsolable. I made my mind up on something I had been putting off, that the voice in my head had been telling me to do.

One night after they had gone to bed in their usual drunken state, I started a fire in the house after removing the battery from the smoke alarm and they both perished. I became angry later when I found out they had both died from smoke Inhalation rather than having to endure the agony of burning to death.

As I was six months short of my sixteenth birthday, the local authority found me a placement in a council run home for teenagers. Cannabis was easily obtained and was much needed, to cope with the grief, and bullying which was rife in the home. My therapy sessions increased to alleviate their fear of what I may attempt to do to myself after losing my mother, stepfather and brother, coupled with my already fragile state of mind. It was their fear, not mine; there was nothing wrong with me.

The grief, the bullying, the therapy sessions, but most of all the voice in my head ordering me to kill the bullies, made my mind up to run away from the home three weeks before my sixteenth birthday.

The first week, I slept on a bench in the local park, the last two nights, leant up against the trunk of a tree, its leaves sheltering me from the rain. I've never been so frightened.

I rummaged among dustbins for food, until I realised there were easier pickings after restaurants had closed and their waste disposed of, before the staff went home.

One night I was caught stealing from one restaurant's bin and as I tried to run, my collar was grabbed.

"Please don't hurt me or call the police. I'll be sent back to the home. I hate it. I've done nothing wrong. I'm just hungry."

Before the chef let go of my collar, he asked me

how long I'd been sleeping rough; how old I was, and was there anyone he could contact for me.

The tears arrived. "The only person who ever loved me is dead now. My mam."

The chef put his arm around me for comfort. "Come back here at the same time each night, except Monday; my night off. I'll leave a bag of food and a hot drink out for you. There's a shed round the corner with very little in it. I'll leave the door unlocked and put a blanket in for you son. You're nearly sixteen now; try to find a job that will get you back on your feet, and stay safe."

"Thank you so much", I said, through the tears, my emotions high.

I watched as he walked back into the kitchens. "I've only met him for five minutes, and he's shown more kindness to me than anyone before in my life."

Seventeen years old, living with friends in a squat. The place is a total mess, not that any of us noticed. We were all drugged up most of the time.

I walk along the pavement avoiding the cracks between the pavers, a game we played as young children has become a matter of life or death. In my mind it got harder as more people filed onto the pavement and I took irrational steps forwards and sideways to dodge the cracks. People noticed and pointed. My breathing intensified, my heart rate increased with the fear of hitting a crack, until I felt another panic attack coming on which forced me off the main street into an alley. I rested until my breathing returned to normal. I remember thinking; *What am I doing? This is stupid. Walk on the damn cracks!* I tried, determined, but couldn't do it.

I got little sleep. Every time I closed my eyes I felt people touch me, my eyes forced quickly back open relieved there was no-one there. I closed them again and immediately felt the dry scaly hands back on me, another disorder re-opening my eyes. It went on for hours. When I did sleep, I saw pictures of Stuart with the skin on his face peeling off before me. Billy, with short stumps where his hands used to be, that he couldn't move at the end of his arms that lay limp at his side; the hands I feared so much. I enjoyed this dream, then realised when I awoke that the flames never hurt them. It was the smoke that killed them and I felt the anger well up inside me, cheated.

CHAPTER ONE

Karina stood in the shadows until a car approached slowly down the back street that had few lights illuminating its path. She stepped forward to the kerb edge, lifting her skirt towards her thigh, a sign to show what she was, and who he would be looking for. Karina was slim with a nice figure, but wore clothing to make sure nobody had the wrong impression of just why she was there.

As the car slowed to where she stood, the window was lowered and conversation started between the two. Karina's head shook, a definite "no" being mouthed, with more conversation following until she nodded in agreement, climbed in, and was driven away.

This was her profession which allowed her to buy the drugs that she badly needed. She no longer questioned the morality of her actions. She needed her fix; full stop. Karina was there night after night, having rid herself two years earlier of her then pimp, who would leave her very little money.

He had come and gone, the same as all the other hangers on before him. Her drug dealing boyfriend who had introduced her to the pimp; the perverted photographer who had removed any last piece of decency she held in her mind, and the club owner who had promised her nightly work in the club, only to be coerced into working in the brothel to the club's rear. All gone now. Only herself to earn for and care for, and inject for.

After returning to her patch she once again raised her skirt, striding towards the kerb edge.

Jack was surprised that he was only merry and not drunk as he walked through the old town, back to his flat, especially as it was his twenty second birthday, having just celebrated it alone in a quiet Coventry backstreet pub. Jack passed Karina, and as he did so nodded to her, slightly smiling. She smiled back, saying hello. Jack stopped and they both got into conversation that sent a warm relaxed feeling inside him, as though he'd known her for years. Twenty minutes into the conversation Karina asked

"Would you like to go with me." She smiled again. "What is it that you'd like me to do for you."

Jack's calmness disappeared, replaced by nervous panic as he realised that she was a prostitute. He was immediately angry with himself for being so stupid as not to notice. He apologised to her saying he had to go, walking briskly away.

Five minutes later he arrived at the entrance to the apartments where he lived, having thought while walking, on their conversation. He stopped but didn't go in, and muttered to himself. "I enjoyed the conversation so much. She seemed so friendly. It's been over a year since I've been with a woman; but a prostitute? I can't do that. Yet she was so easy to talk to. No airs or graces."

Jack walked back through the streets towards her, feeling, somehow fearing that she would no longer be there; off perhaps in some punter's car. He questioned himself as he went. He turned the corner. She was still there. She looked so good.

"I'm sorry I dashed off."

"Don't worry. It's not a problem." She replied.

"I enjoyed talking with you. Could we talk some more?" Jack asked.

"I also enjoyed your company but we both know why I'm here. I liked it because you didn't realise what I do for a living. It was good relaxed conversation. The people who usually stop and talk understand what I do and their conversation is not nearly so nice, normally just business like. Even when they try to be friendly, mostly it's just a very uncomfortable front that a child could see through. I think most of them don't like themselves very much for what they do, making them like me even less."

"How long have you been doing this for?"--"I'm sorry. It's not my business, I shouldn't have asked." Jack quickly added.

"Stop apologising Jack. Although I'm now sorry. I need to be seen here by myself, as much as I would like to carry on chatting."

"Karina I'm lonely and would like to talk some more. Would you care to come back to my flat for a coffee?"

Karina stared at him with raised eyebrows, a smile on her face.

Jack realised what the look meant. "I'll pay the

going rate but I just want to talk."

They talked and talked right through the night, until Karina said that she had to go home to get some rest. They arranged to meet a few days later which soon became a regular arrangement.

At Jack's flat during their second week of seeing each other Karina looked deeply into Jacks eyes.

"Jack there's something different about you and I know this might sound stupid, especially as you know what I do, but can we take things really slowly as I'm scared if we start having sex too soon I'll just think of you as a client, and I would hate that. We're both capable of so much more and I feel that we could really have something special here."

Jack took Karina's hands into his own and pulled her to him. "I'll never make any demands of you. I'll wait until you tell me that you're ready."

They kissed passionately, something she never allowed any punter to do.

After they had been seeing each other for six weeks Jack asked her to move in with him but she felt it was too early, and for him to be patient a little longer. After a further two weeks she turned up at his flat crying.   "Jack I'm sorry. I've been keeping something from you. I've been threatened with the bailiffs. I can't pay my rent and my landlord wants me out if I don't pay the arrears by tomorrow. I hate to ask, but is there any way you could lend me the money?"

"How much do you owe?"

"Four hundred pounds. I didn't want to ask. I"ve been so stressed. I'll pay you back. I promise."

"Karina I've only got three hundred pounds that I keep by for emergencies, but you can have it. You know I'm on benefits and by the time I've paid everything out it only leaves about thirty pounds spare each week."

Jack never noticed her eyes light up. "Thank you so much Jack. I'm sure that will take the pressure off."

"Karina, please move in with me. It makes so much sense. I won't take any money from you, and you'll have so much more spare cash."

"Jack I am coming round to the idea, but I need a little more time."

He went to his bedroom and came back with her money. She hugged him tightly. "I won't forget this." she promised.

A week later she turned up again begging for twenty pounds, which, after a long look at her, he took it from his wallet. The following week she asked for fifteen pounds.

"Karina I promised myself I would never ask what money you made from your work, but the problem's got to be with the amount of money you're spending on drugs. Please, please let me help you to come away from them. I think you're health will suffer because of them and you'll have so much more money left, although your health is the only thing I care about."

"I only want fifteen quid." she snapped.

Reluctantly he once again gave in.

Once she had it in her purse, she gave him a scowling look." I'm fed up with you continually telling me to come off the drugs. I can stop any time I want. I enjoy it, and it helps me get through what I do."

"But I could really help." He replied.

"Here we go again. I'm glad I haven't moved

in. I don't know if this is going to work between us."

"Karina don't finish. I'm begging you. I promise I won't ask again."
She turned round and walked out the door. "I'll think about it." She mouthed, without turning to look at him, a glib look stretched across her face.

The following day Karina rang Jack to apologise. "I know we've got something special and I promise that at some point I will move in with you, but it isn't the right time just yet."

"When you're ready. I'll never put any pressure on you." Jack replied.

Karina blew a kiss down the phone, then hung up.

CHAPTER TWO

I celebrated my twenty seventh birthday by myself. Karina, three years earlier had been so cruelly taken from me. Alone in this world with only memories left to torture me. I needed her so badly. I had to try again. I lit a candle at either end of the mantelpiece after lining Karina's photographs along it. I switched off the main light and played her favourite C.D., humming along to the lyrics as I held on tightly to her favourite watch with one hand as I put the tablets to my mouth with the other. I pictured her in my mind; pictured us both together again as I raised the water to my lips.

As I became drowsier the music's rhythm was interrupted by shouting that I could vaguely hear.

"Jack what the hell have you done? Have you taken the full bottle? Talk to me."

The ambulance sped through the blackness

of the night, its blinding blue light scattering people from its path. Jack's new neighbour had discovered his still body as he had called round to talk to Jack, the empty pill bottle at Jack's side.

The paramedic worked feverishly in the back of the ambulance to bring Jack out of his unconscious state and on arrival at the hospital, he was rushed into a cubicle as two doctors took over in an attempt to resuscitate him. The lines on the heart monitor zig-zagged up and down until a flat line replaced the ripples, in conjunction with a low humming sound; the noise of near death.

Jacks eyes hadn't reopened, yet unconsciously he was the only one in the room aware of a bright light's existence as it came to him from the top corner of the room swallowing him in its path, before withdrawing to the ceiling and then beyond. Jack watched the doctors from above working on his lifeless body as he rose further upwards, watching them desperately trying to bring him round.

Travelling within the light he was aware of a distant unrecognisable figure that gradually became clearer as it drew closer. It was Karina with brilliant light all around her but her arms didn't open to welcome Jack to her; her smile wasn't there, now only consigned to memory. He held out his own arms, hoping to entwine with hers, as a distant cry tried to break into his mind,one that was unintelligible in its muffled form. He didn't care as he drew closer to the only place that he wanted to be. He was inches away from Karina's clasped hands when the cry came again. "Stand clear,"and seconds later the normal pattern of waves appeared on the heart monitor.

"He's back with us" came the cry as the doctors once again began working on Jack, saving another patient knowing that once he had fully recovered physically, different doctors would have to work their magic, delving into his mind in an effort to keep Jack from trying again.

The following morning he lay still in the hospital bed, staring at the ceiling in the small room where, alone, he was angry at being taken away from Karina for a second time when he was so close to her, though somehow the urgency to be with her at this moment was nowhere near as great as it had been the previous day, yet he couldn't understand why. One of the doctors who had helped save him came through to see him, a small, plump, bald headed man "How are you feeling this morning? A lot better I hope."

"I suppose I should thank you for saving my life" Jack said without smiling.

CHAPTER THREE

The following year appeared to pass so quickly, yet equally for Jack, time also seemed to stand still. He paced up and down, occasionally swiping ornaments from the table or windowsill as he passed, not hearing them crack into tiny fragments, his mind in another world; the anger one minute upon his face, replaced by sorrow the next. He was in a bad place, negative thoughts abounding, questioning the point of continuing to live. He picked Karina's jumper up from his armchair, holding it into his face, breathing in deeply, attempting to drown himself in her natural fragrance, not realising that the aroma had long disappeared. It was of his own making; too many tears making the sweater damp, smelling more fusty than of Karina, although Jack didn't realise as he was living in that fusty atmosphere day in, day out; a mixture of clothing in desperate need of laundering combined with a rancid body odour. He strode through the door in great need of fresh air, in even greater need of fresh thoughts.

He stood towards the bottom of his garden looking into the sky, one hand flattened across the top of his forehead shielding his eyes against the midday sun that fleetingly flickered through the leaves of the surrounding trees as the gentle breeze played on them, allowing perfect vision for several seconds; the next, blinded by the glare. He was watching the birds. In his other hand, a plate carrying yesterdays leftovers was tipped, allowing the food to drop onto the path that was barely visible, covered by a blend of overgrown grass and weeds. Jack felt safe outside; inside the house, his mind was trapped in its own dungeon, a mixture of his ongoing sorrow regarding Karina coupled with his worsening obsessive compulsive disorder.

The sky was clear except for one small cloud that drifted slowly above the trees. His hand left his forehead in shock, his index finger pointing unbelievingly towards the cloud. "There!" He stood frozen, all concentration fixed onto the cloud. "There it is again, Karina's face; it's her; I can plainly see her." The plate, without notice slipped from his other hand, until the crack on the concrete broke his stare. He immediately looked back up, desperate once again to see Karina, but the cloud's shape had changed. He looked harder until the sun blinded him, and disappointed, he turned to walk away as his depression started to kick in as it did most days, remembering her, remembering the times that would never be again.

He walked back down the path towards the house. "They've done it again!," he said angrily to himself. Sprayed in paint on the brickwork above the window it read:

INDIGNATION. JUDGEMENT AWAITS.

Below the window, painted in the same manner were the words

THE OMNIPOTENT.

Sprayed in larger lettering across the window Itself was the devils name.

SATAN.

Jack was angry as it was the second time in a month that the vandals had struck without a sound, and it had been regularly painted in the same place on and off for the last year. The words were identical each time. He slammed the door behind him, causing the long dried flaking paint to fall from it, floating down, settling itself on the grassy path that blended in with the green mould that was taking a hold on the lower brickwork of the house. Inside the kitchen he passed pots, unwashed for days, kicking discarded food wrappers out of his way and slumped into an easy chair in the living room, thrusting thousands of particles of dust into the air, shimmering in the sunlight as they drifted back down to resettle. The dust was everywhere, thickly across his television screen, layered over the glass coffee table, so dense it no longer allowed a reflection. Six mugs stood on the table, each holding varying amounts of long discarded tea, the dust hiding the green that had engulfed the milk.

Out of view were the many boxes of unopened medication that had been prescribed for daily use but hadn't been taken for months. His beard wasn't grown by choice, it merely appeared as a result of his laziness coupled with his non-existent personal hygiene.

Jack never smiled, always a sombre look on

his face, but no-one could second guess the continual woes that his fragile mind believed were all around him. He had no friends except for Ricky Gill, who shared his house and who was always there in times of trouble.

Jack had been allowed home following his discharge from The Hawthorns mental health facility, after the unit's psychiatrists had witnessed a continuing gradual improvement to the point they felt that he no longer posed a threat to himself, never having been a risk to others. He had been sectioned after twice attempting suicide amid concern surrounding his pre-existing mental health issues.

When Jack had been discharged from the mental health assessment unit, one of the first things that he did was to visit a local church, something he'd never done in his life. He walked slowly into the church, looking all around him as he went. He saw the carvings above him that stretched across the ceiling, finishing above the alter. He had seen the stained glass windows from the outside but stood in silent awe as he marvelled over their beauty with the light cascading through them and he felt a strange sense of belonging. The minister walked over to him.

"Thanks for seeing me. I have never been a religious man believing in an afterlife; always of the opinion that this life was for now and once gone, it had gone. I know now for certain that is not the case and ask for your guidance to help me find the Lord."

"My son I am so pleased that you have seen the light and I will help you in any way that I can. What happened in your life to so convincingly lead you to the right path?"

"Father I have sinned by attempting to take my own life but you said the right words `seen the light`. That was exactly what happened to me. I had an out of body experience and was close to death. A ray of light took me into it and raised me higher to a totally relaxed plane where I found Karina waiting, who not so long ago was taken from me. When I came around I wondered if my mind had been playing tricks and if I only felt It had happened because I was so desperate to be back with her, but I know beyond any doubt that for a few brief seconds we were back together, as one day we will be."

Jack became a regular churchgoer where a

strength from his faith grew in him, but pulling him in another direction was his uncontrollable depression, although his friend Ricky would always be there to help and support him. Jack had never really held a job down due mainly to his repeated depressive bouts and he never had any hobbies apart from the continuous hours of reading his bible, sometimes out aloud.-----"and forgive us our trespasses, as we forgive those who trespass against us and lead us not into temptation, but deliver us from evil. For thine is the kingdom, the power and the glory, for ever and ever. Amen."

He opened his eyes and drew a cross over his chest with his fingers and then looked up to the mantelpiece where a large gold frame held his favourite picture of his beloved Karina. The tears flowed away from him as the sadness enveloped him once again. He rose to his feet clearing his eyes, rubbing them with his hands as he walked over to the fireplace to get a closer look at the woman he would never see again in this life.

He picked the photograph up from the mantel and pressed it to his chest before raising it to his lips to kiss her as if she was in his presence, before placing it gently back down, looking all around him. Photographs and memorabilia adorned the walls and shelves; his shrine to Karina. The tears returned.

"Jack I know it's hard even though it's been around four years now, but eventually it will get easier. She loved you too you know and is most likely watching over you right now.

"But Ricky why won't she allow me to join her? She must know I've tried, but she keeps stopping me----or perhaps it's God. I'm so sorry my Lord. I know my life is not my own to take and although I hurt so much I will try to find the strength to resist." He started his breathing exercises that his doctor had shown him for his periodic panic attacks until he fully settled back down, and in an attempt to divert his thoughts he picked up the local newspaper, The Evening Star, but on page seven he shook his head in disgust at the personal advertisements that jumped out at him.

"ROXY and JULIE. Mobile massage parlour. Free second session. Let us blow your mind away. God forgive them."

`DISCREET escort agency. New girls to our team. Many nationalities. Many pleasures just a phone call away. `

"SAMANTHA. Attractive model. Anything considered. Distance no object. Why should these vulnerable women be exploited and allowed to degrade themselves by a newspaper that has no moral standards?, instead only a need for advertising revenue regardless of any consequence. Whoever sanctions these advertisements must be without any morals."

"They're not vulnerable. They're all whores. You should know."

"Shut up Ricky." Jacks thoughts returned to Karina. " It's been nearly four years since she left me and the people who were collectively responsible for her disreputable life and eventual death still walk around freely, going about their sordid businesses driving other poor souls down the road to ruin. Not one of them will have Karina on their conscience. They probably wouldn't even remember her name or recognise her photograph if shown it. Why should these personal advertisements even be allowed? Societies standards are slowly being eroded and it will only get progressively worse." Jacks mouth twisted with anger. "I won't allow it!" he screamed out aloud. "I will no longer stand idly by and watch as more of these lost women are manipulated by greedy parasites as Karina was until she passed the point of no return."

"You're a hypocrite. You continually blame others for your wife's demise. I've listened to it endlessly without speaking up. You talk about revenge on the people you blame, calling these women innocent victims. They're equally as bad. They're just as guilty, although you won't put Karina in that bracket because she was your wife. You allow it to cloud your judgement."

Jack stormed out of the room, angry but silent. He wanted to give his friend a volley of verbal abuse but managed to keep it in. He stood in the hallway staring into the mirror, thinking of Karina and how he missed her so much. He pushed his hands through his hair imagining that they were Karina's hands, knowing he would never have that feeling again. Jack's sleeves dropped a short way down his arms revealing slowly healing scars across both wrists where he had attempted to take his own life. Most people that knew him felt that it was just a cry for help. It wasn't. Jack really wanted to die to be back with her. He couldn't get over Karina.

He remembered holding her closely as she poured out her heart about her early life. A stepfather who regularly gave her a thrashing. The times she cried herself to sleep as a young child, left by her mother and stepfather to go out, never knowing if they had returned home until she had awoken the next morning, sometimes gone for days at a time, having to fend for herself. The love she craved. The love she had to give. He'd packed her suitcase on her sixteenth birthday; told her to make her own way in life, then ungraciously kicked her out. Karina's mother, eyes wide with fear, wanting to shout out, too scared to do so, with her hand held to her mouth attempting to stop the sobbing as she was pushed back into the house. Her upbringing appeared identical to his own and he shared her pain. Karina was heartbroken when two years later she learnt of her mother's death from a friend, a week after the funeral had taken place.

Jack walked back into the room. "Ricky you don't understand. You don't know what it feels like so I'm going to tell you everything even though you never knew Karina. When, after seven weeks down the line I asked her to stop working the streets, she explained it was the only way she could raise the money for her drugs. She had no other source of income and I wasn't working. I begged her to get help to stop the drug taking but she would only shrug and walk away. After several disagreements we called the relationship off. I lasted less than a week before I begged her to see me again. Ricky I couldn't live without her. She told me that she loved me but still had to work to feed her drug habit. She couldn't emphasise enough that no client meant anything to her. It was only an act, and I was the one she would always come home to."

Jack walked across to the mantle, took the framed photograph of Karina from it and stared lovingly into it. "Because of my love for her I accepted the situation, and although never comfortable with it, it became less of an issue with time, although I begged time and again to let me help her come off the drugs".

Jack looked up but Ricky had quietly left the room. He and Ricky had become close friends shortly after Karina's death and over time had become Inseparable. He was a rock and Jack wouldn't do anything that might upset the friendship, although both had widely different views on many subjects that generated fiery confrontation on many occasions. If the arguments got out of hand, rather than revert to a physical level Jack always walked away to cool off. Jack would not lose this argument. He knew Ricky was wrong. "I will not hurt who I consider to be the victims, the pawns, but I have left it too long. Karina will be avenged. The parasites will all pay. I'll devise a plan; think long and hard in advance of any eventualities or pitfalls to make certain that I leave no clue allowing the police to detect me until all Karina's enemies have been punished".

As usual with Jack, positive thoughts immediately turned to the negative, his emotions a reflection on his minds fragility as he buried his head in his hands.

"Oh my Lord please forgive me. I am so tormented. I know what I am considering is so wrong but they are sinners who continue to debase your flock. I know what they deserve yet know I cannot kill them."

"But I can."

Jack spun around unaware that Ricky had returned or heard him talking aloud.

"I know the pain you are going through, though my feelings differ to yours and the women that you feel a need to protect. I still share your condemnation of those who drove Karina's downfall and I will help you to be rid of them. I know your religious beliefs will not allow you to kill. I have none and will do what's needed. We are like brothers and I can no longer stand by knowing the pain and anguish that your mind endures. As far as I am concerned it is an eye for an eye, but Jack, if you are serious, then you have to get a grip of yourself; think more clearly; regain a pride in yourself with your appearance; lose the beard; have your hair cut and start washing both yourself and your clothing once again. Only when you have straightened yourself out will you be able to set your mind to the tasks that lay ahead."

CHAPTER FOUR

Dave Arnold went straight to the fridge for a beer after letting himself in. He sunk his huge frame into his favourite armchair forcing the sides of the cushion to bellow outwards near to bursting. The constant years of only sitting at his desk or driving his car without any form of exercise had taken it's toll on his appearance but although it slowed his movement down physically, it never affected his speed in judgement of thought. It was an attribute that had gained him a quick rise through the ranks to his present position of Detective Chief Inspector, although not all of his colleagues shared the view that it was deserved.

"You're early today." A voice shouted from the bathroom.

"Not much happening down at the station; at least nothing to get your teeth into."

His wife Fiona entered the living room, a towel

pulled snugly around her curvaceous figure, a smaller one wrapped around her head. "Even so, you're never usually in before seven p.m."

"I wanted to make certain that you were okay after your dialysis. I know it's not as straightforward as it used to be. I wanted to take you to the hospital today but as Simon was through from York I thought it best to give you both some space."

"He left for home an hour ago Dave. He asked me to reconsider his earlier offer of accepting one of his kidneys as it would limit the chances of rejection. I can't do it. I know one will come along eventually, although the specialist warned me that my arteries are starting to harden and to take my son's offer seriously as a much longer delay might make an operation impossible to perform."

Her husband held her tightly for comfort.

Dave and Fiona had been together for twenty years and married for ten of them. Simon was fifteen when they moved in together and like any teenager, was protective towards his mother, but gradually drew closer to Dave and by the time Simon left home to study in York, was happy for his mother with Dave in her life.

After he finished university, Simon started working in York where he eventually settled, seeing his mother four or five times a year.

Dave's job grew more demanding as he rose through the ranks, but they both managed two, sometimes three holidays abroad each year, with occasional weekends away, but with his last promotion to Detective Chief Inspector four years earlier, coupled with Fiona's health issues, the holidays were curtailed. Her kidney problem had grown worse and now required regular dialysis.

CHAPTER FIVE

Four years earlier Jack had taken out his favourite photographs and memorabilia that Karina possessed, consigning the rest of her possessions into seven manageable sized cardboard boxes which he stored In the attic. He took them down one by one. Wiping away the dust, meticulously searching through them, he remembered seeing a photo of Karina's mother and stepfather, taken when Karina was fifteen, with their address on the back. Sifting his way through the first box he came across a glittering angel that Karina had kept after her mother had taken the Christmas tree down one year: *Her happy time as she had described it. Not many happy times* Jack reflected, *and certainly no angel looking over her.*

He moved onto the next box and found what he was looking for halfway down. Jack eyed her stepfather with hatred. "The people I will punish for causing Karina's downward spiral will all lose their lives, but not this sinner; I will find a punishment where his agony is continuous."

After checking for his name and address in the telephone directory he was unable to find it and so the following day he drove through to Birmingham to see if Karina's stepfather still lived at the same address.

He knew where it was having lived close by himself many years earlier. He parked In between the cars that lined the avenue remaining unnoticed, thirty metres away from the location penned on the back of the photograph. The avenue of pre-war houses in blocks of twenty, had a wide alleyway at the end of each block with many more cars parked down them.

The area was semi-derelict with dozens of properties boarded up and many with for sale notices, only emphasising the dereliction. There was an acrid smell in the air, the area behind the street being an old business park. *It never smelt as bad when I lived nearby.* Out of the eight units, only two still operated; one a small paint manufacturer, the other a tannery. Jack wondered how anyone could live there with the stench they now gave off. After a two hour wait someone emerged through the front door and walked towards Jack's parked car turning off into one of the alleys. "It's him! John Stamp. He still lives here; good."

Two minutes later he drove out in an old black Mondeo estate that had wide red stripes running along the full length of both sides. Jack didn't follow him; there was time enough for that. This would be a prolonged stake out with all of his comings and goings observed, but just as important, time had to be spent near to his house watching for any movement to ascertain if anyone else lived there. When the plan was finally devised and initiated, he had to be certain of Stamp's routine. So certain that no-one could substantiate any possible alibi.

Each night Stamp arrived back home around nine thirty. On the third night Jack returned to the alley where stamp's car was parked and at two a.m. quietly aided by the darkness, unscrewed the front registration plate from the Mondeo.

After the first week he started checking car sales on the internet, away from the Birmingham area, searching for a black Mondeo estate, until five days later he located one in Leeds. Jack purchased it and later visited a graphic design shop buying thin magnetic strip as well as a sheet of bright red adhesive vinyl.

The next day, after feeling assured that Stamp lived alone, Jack started following him. Every day was the same; Stamp drove to a small fishing lake fifteen miles outside of Birmingham. He parked his car and walked several hundred metres to set up at what must have been a favourite spot, and he stayed there each day until nine in the evening, hardly ever another angler there.

After two weeks of tailing him Jack felt confident enough to initiate his plan of action knowing Stamp's routine. That night Jack returned to the alley to remove the rear registration plate, the front one having been replaced earlier.

John Stamp's build was similar to Jacks, and most days Stamp had worn the same overlong bright red chunky jumper that his long brown unkempt hair hung over, and in his unshaven state gave the impression that he might smell.

Jack immediately became embarrassed with his thoughts, realising that not so very long ago he was that same person with his lack of personal hygiene.

After hours of searching different clothing retailers without success for a similar red jumper to Stamp's he came across one by chance in a charity shop. The long brown wig proved no problem to buy.

The following day, dressed in his jumper, wig and dark glasses to look like Stamp, Jack sat in his newly acquired Mondeo complete with Stamp's registration plates, and attached to both sides of the car, the magnetic strips bearing the red vinyl. He was parked in the Evening Star's car park positioned in between two CCTV cameras, where he waited for two hours. He repeated this daily but on the fourth day he parked close to a car that was in a reserved bay with Lynn Tudor boldly written on the wall.

Lynn Tudor walked out of the editor's office a happy woman after a trial run of reporting on several local news events, to the editor's total satisfaction. She had long been qualified as a journalist, but for twelve years had run the advertising section of the local newspaper, the Evening Star. Her happy disposition made for a contented team of tele-sales staff under her, and she was well liked by everyone, but she was ready for a new challenge. Tudor was thirty four, blonde and a little overweight. Her personality generated many admirers and requests for dates. She always refused them. Her marriage had ended three years earlier and had initially left her devastated. As yet, although completely over her ex husband, she was in no mind to get involved or close to anyone. Lynn was happy in her own space, living in a secluded countryside cottage, a short drive out of Coventry with only her dog and two cats for company; just the way she wanted it. She felt as happy in life at this moment as she had at any time and walked across to her car thinking only of her promotion.

Lynn Tudor had been responsible for the personal advertisements section when Karina first advertised herself.

As he had many times before, Jack once again covered the whole operation in his mind that they were about to undertake to make doubly certain that nothing had been overlooked; that no clue of any type could be left by chance or misfortune.

Tudor climbed into the car in her space. Jack followed her to make certain that the car arrived at one of the twelve addresses registered under the name Tudor in the telephone directory. He had never seen her before and couldn't afford to get the wrong person as the consequence of her actions was too severe to serve on someone mistakenly.

After following her for twenty minutes through the one o' clock rush hour traffic, she drove out of the city into the countryside, where fifteen miles further on the car pulled into the driveway of a remote detached cottage on Wilby Lane, which address was entered in the directory.

Jack drove on by so as not to arouse any suspicion. He parked his car a short way off, and walked back around the bend. He had a full view of her home, out of sight himself, behind the hedgerow.

Tudor's nearest neighbour was a half mile back down the narrow lane. *Her cottage was built many years ago*, thought Jack, the walls constructed from solid stone "Nice car! Nice cottage!, but not a nice person. No different to all the other sinners, profiteering from the desperate situation of others, who, needing so many things, they eventually sell their bodies. Tudor gave them the means to do so with a disregard for any moral responsibility. She must answer to God."

After an hour she emerged with a small poodle following closely behind where she walked a short distance along the lane before entering a wooded area, not returning for twenty five minutes, just before it started getting dusky.

Once back in the cottage the lights were turned on before she moved across the room to draw the curtains closely watched all the way by Jack until the last chink of light disappeared behind them.

"She'll be making herself comfortable now, settling down onto her soft sofa as the wood in her open fire crackles and spits, bursting into a bright flame, the dog laid at her feet in her expensive cottage. Luxuries, all afforded by her earnings brought about by the suffering of others." Jack muttered uncontrollably to himself. He kicked the ground hard in anger.

He made a daily trip for a week carefully following her into the woods to check her movements and discovered that she stuck to the same path on each occasion. On the third day when she had entered the wood, Jack dressed in a balaclava, overall and wearing gloves walked into the driveway of the cottage and tried Tudor's car door; it was unlocked. On the driver's seat he found blonde hairs which he carefully placed into a plastic money bag before returning to his viewing position.

On the following day when Tudor was at work he returned to her cottage where he had noticed a patch of mud, still soft, close to her driveway. He went to the boot of his car and took out a plastic carrier bag and walked around to the mud, emptying the carrier's contents over it. A dead hedgehog fell from the bag landing in the middle of the mud and after returning to his car, he drove over both the mud and hedgehog, making certain that the tyre left it's track in the mud along with the squashed hedgehog before he drove half a mile down the lane where he stopped and replaced the bloodied wheel with the spare tyre. He carefully placed the bloodied wheel into a heavy duty refuse bag before putting it into his boot.

Quietly, after midnight in the dimly lit alleyway near to Stamp's house, he jacked Stamp's car up and swapped his near side front wheel for the bloodied one.

The following morning, after he delivered his own Mondeo to a pre-arranged buyer in Nottingham, Jack arrived back to destroy the registration plates, red vinyl magnetic strips, red jumper and wig before driving in his Fiat Punto through to the lake to make certain that Stamp was there alone as usual. Parked close to the fishing lake Jack walked across to Stamps car dressed in the same manner as the day before. He was out of view of Stamp and tried his door, pleased to find it unlocked, whereby he placed Tudor's hairs from his plastic money bag onto the back of the drivers seat and several onto the floor.

The following afternoon with his pulse racing, Ricky climbed out of the car, put on a new pair of gloves, removed the balaclava from its wrapper and slipped it over his head carefully placing both wrappings into a bin liner. He then removed the new dark blue nylon overalls from their bag and quickly climbed into them after placing the empty bag into the bin liner.

He then proceeded to put his new trainers on, straight from the box before placing the slippers into the box that he had stepped from the car in. The shoe box went into the bin liner along with the protective wrapper from his newly acquired kitchen knife which he slid into the rule pocket of his overalls. He waited tentatively behind a large oak tree deep in the wood on Tudors usual path. As he heard her approach, his adrenalin pumped vigorously with fear and apprehension, the cold sweat was pouring from him while his hands shook uncontrollably, but he would not back out now for Karina's sake.

She turned the corner, the dog lagging behind, sniffing at another tree's base and walked on in her usual pace knowing that the poodle would catch up, but as she passed the oak tree Tudor fell to the ground clutching her throat, slashed in one quick sweep of the razor sharp knife. Ricky looked down at her, the blood pouring in even pulsating spurts away from her as she desperately tried to catch her breath.

"Poor bastard. You didn't deserve to die. If it had been left up to me, I would have let you live, but Jack insisted that you be the first." He took out an unused mobile phone and took a picture of the person first in line leading to the downfall of Karina and with a last glance he walked away leaving the poodle sniffing and whimpering around her limp body.

Back at the car he carefully put the knife into the shoe box inside the bin liner, removed his overalls, shirt and trousers also placing them into the liner. Stood in just his shorts and trainers he did the same with the balaclava and gloves before sliding the first liner into a second bin liner to make certain that any unseen fibres from his clothing that could be on the outside of the original liner could not cling to the car's upholstery. He then stepped out of his trainers straight into the car, without touching the ground, before reaching through the door to place the trainers with the rest of his attire. Ricky slipped his spare shoes on after his shirt and trousers.

Jack looked directly ahead not turning to face Ricky, and drove calmly away to destroy the bin liner and contents. "In the morning I'll drive through to Leicester, where I've identified two separate companies that specialise in part worn tyres, in case of any tracks left behind in the Lane, changing the two rear tyres at the first one, the front tyres at the second, explaining that I felt a slight skid and wasn't prepared to take any chances." The rest of the drive home was made in complete silence,

Jack never shifted his gaze from the road. He knew that his decision to be rid of Lynn Tudor would save her soul from eternal damnation and in the light of knowledge that now guided him he knew that others yet to follow would have salvation in the name of Karina.

CHAPTER SIX

The following afternoon the Evening Star received a photo from Jack's mobile of Lynn Tudor, her face spattered in blood. They immediately called the police and a patrol car was at her cottage within fifteen minutes only to find the poodle sat at the door with bloodstained fur. Her body was located twenty minutes later in the woods.

D.C.I. Dave Arnold was appointed in charge of the investigation, and as a mobile unit was being made ready to transport to the front of the cottage, he assembled his team to bring everyone up to date with the case. " Sarah take a colleague and go down to the Evening Star's office to interview her colleagues to get an idea of how they all got along and also to see if they knew of any relationships that she may have been involved in. Find out who the next of kin were. This is going to blow up fast and we need to get them informed. Kate I want you to go to their offices and bring all the CCTV footage back with you to start scanning it immediately. Apparently the cottage is quite remote: never the less I'm sending two officers to visit her nearest neighbours to see what they can find out and also see if there are any local shops or pub or even a church in the area where people congregate, to see if anyone had any kind of an inkling of something not being quite right. We'll visit the crime scene before any further decisions are made on the way forward with the investigation. The pathologist is already on his way down and the lane has been blocked off so no-one can disturb the crime scene and forensics are down there now."

After Dave Arnold's arrival to the murder scene he appointed a team to conduct a fingertip search, side by side through the wooded area and lane. He stopped outside the cottage and looked around him. An area surrounded by trees, eerily quiet with the majority of birds having flown south for the Winter. It was a clear and crisp November morning. He could understand someone choosing to live in such an idyllic setting, having temporarily escaped from what would have been a manic job in the hustle and bustle of every day city life. He realised he had just run his own job description through his mind and felt a degree of jealousy.

Arnold turned off his thoughts and switched his police head back on. The weather had been dry for over a day which was ideal from the point of not losing any clues that may have been left behind. Close to the cottage driveway, the tyre track was discovered, imprinted into a patch of dry mud. Also next to the impression lay the remains of the squashed hedgehog, with its blood in the tyre track. As the D.C.I. was about to enter the cottage his mobile rang.

"Dave it's Chief Superintendent Burns here: I can't believe it. Lynn Tudor is sergeant Hopewell's daughter. I've just sent him home in a patrol car in an obvious state of shock. I didn't know what to say to him."

After a stunned silence he replied. "I'll go and see Tom later when I've got things up and running here. I'm gutted for him; Her name never clicked with me as Lynn retained her married name after her divorce three years ago. We'll find this bastard. She was all Tom had after losing his wife last year. I don't know if he'll be able to take it".

After he hung up the D.C.I. immediately brought Lynn's face into his mind. He shook his head in disbelief. He would be seeing her in minutes laid out dead between the trees. He carefully strode across the woodland in his protective suit to avoid any contamination of the murder scene. The pathologist had finished his work there and the body was ready to be moved to the morgue, all photographs taken. Dave Arnold cringed when he saw her; "Poor Lynn, and God help Tom. Nobody deserves this."

After a word with forensics who were combing the cottage area he set off to see the victim's father knowing that for the first time in charge of four murder cases, he would be lost for words.

The closed circuit television tapes from the newspaper's office were played and replayed by D.C. Kate Jones, with the cars in the car park accounted for, excepting for three. Out of these it was realised that a Mondeo had been parked for four consecutive days, each time for several hours with the driver remaining in his car, although, even with these shots fully blown up, a full likeness of the drivers face wasn't as clear as the police would have liked, it gave them a reasonable enough closeness that might allow identification if the driver could be found. On the last day of the Mondeo being parked, it was close to Lynn Tudor's car and when she pulled out the Mondeo followed her.

The car was registered to a John Stamp and unable to find him at his home, the police questioned his neighbours, with one remembering having seen him leave earlier in the day carrying a holdall.

The following morning at the press conference the D.C.I. invited questions after his introductory statement of facts.

"Was there any motive for the killing?" asked a reporter from the Sun.

"None that we are aware of."

"You say a photograph of the dead woman was sent to the newspaper where she worked. How was it sent?"

"I have nothing to add to that at this moment in time." Arnold pointed in turn to different reporters, each one eager to fire questions.

"Was she well liked at her place of work?" enquired another.

"We are establishing her working relationship with her colleagues as we speak. A team of detectives are with them now and they will also be offered counselling should it be required."

"Was there any sexual motive involved?"

"None what-so-ever."

"Was anything stolen from her home?" the same reporter added before the D.C.I. could point to someone else.

" No. her cottage was locked, the keys still in her coat pocket."

"With the newspaper being contacted it was obviously not a random killing knowing where she worked. Have you any theories on that point?"

"Not at present; people are still being interviewed. I would ask for a John Stamp to contact us as he may have unknowingly witnessed something. He drives a black Mondeo estate with red stripes down both sides of the car. The cars registration is R 698 GTD. If he would come forward, he may be able to assist us. If anyone sees a car of this description, would they please contact the police. The enquiry is only hours old. As soon as we have any further information we will let you know. Thank you gentlemen."

Jack watched the main evening news as the murder story was being covered. The reporter was close to the wood where the body had been discovered and after outlining the story, it switched back to the studio where her father was interviewed. Fighting back tears, he made a personal plea for anyone with any information to come forward saying she never hurt a fly.

"Never hurt a fucking fly. Is he stupid? He must have known what her job consisted of. She was the first in a line of uncaring people involved in Karina's downfall. Perhaps not as instrumental as some but guilty none-the-less. He's a copper. He would have known what she did was wrong and could have persuaded her to stop or change her job. It could have saved her from herself. Now I've had to save her in the eyes of the lord."

CHAPTER SEVEN

Tom Hopewell was deep in thought, his Patterdale terrier stretched out across his legs enjoying his master nonchalantly tickling its stomach. Tom was alone, no one to turn to for support, his only relative a nephew who lived in Australia and there had been no contact for several years. Lynn's face was all he could see until the knock at his door broke his hypnotic like trance, helped by Blackie's barking as he instantly jumped from Toms lap. On opening the door he beckoned his next door neighbour through.

"Thanks for coming Jean; I've got Blackie's things ready, his bed and food. I'll only be gone a few days."

"Tom it's no problem. I've told you before that we'll look after Blackie any time you want us to. He's a smashing little dog and he's really taken to David who continually begs his father and me to get him a similar dog. Tom I don't know what to say. I can't find the words but you know if there's anything that you need or I can do, you've only to ask."

"I know" he replied.

Tom gave Blackie a tight hug which drew a strange look from his neighbour, before he closed the door behind them and returned to his lounge. After sitting staring at the wall for a further half hour he went across to his video recorder and slotted in the first cassette from when Lynn was only three years old.

During the morning he played out another five tapes, laughing and remembering, later crying and remembering. He took a photograph album from a drawer and slowly turned the pages. A smile broke onto his face as he saw his wife Irene laughing with Lynn as they sat next to a swimming pool while on holiday in Greece. The photo was taken four years earlier on what proved to be their last holiday together.

With that thought firmly in his mind, he took a deep breath and did to himself the act that he felt would reunite the whole family once again. The knife slipped from his grasp, its blade coated in crimson as he sat back in his chair looking at the three of them In happier times that was hung above the fireplace. He glanced across to Blackies picture. "I'm glad Blackie will have a good home; too energetic for me but a great companion for eleven year old David."

His peaceful exit was abruptly interrupted as the dog bounded through the door that must not have been latched properly as he had let his neighbour out. Jean followed on close behind and immediately saw the blood. "Oh my God; Tom what have you done?"

"Jean I'm sorry, I didn't mean for you to find me. I must go to them, there's nothing here for me now.Please just leave as you came and let me slip quietly away."

To see the blood dripping from Tom's wrists proved too much and she immediately called for an ambulance, before applying tightly knotted tea towels to both arms in an attempt to stop the flow of blood. Tom tried to resist but was too weak to put up much of a struggle. The ambulance quickly arrived and rushed him off to the hospital a mile away.

The morning mail arrived at police headquarters, with a letter posted within the Coventry area addressed to D.C.I. Arnold. It contained a note stencilled in pencil onto plain paper which read:

FIND THE CONNECTION IF YOU CAN

TO THE REMNANTS OF A BROKEN MAN

WHO MUST YET KILL FIVE TIMES MORE

TO AVENGE THE ONE THAT HE ADORED   6
-- 1

Accompanying the note was a cut out section of the personal advertisements from the Evening Star which outlined massage parlours and escort agencies.

The note and envelope were immediately bagged up and sent to the Forensic Science Service in Birmingham.

"We now know for certain that the murder was premeditated and not random. Lynn Tudor was responsible for the final approval of all advertisements. Now for the letter. If the note's correct he's contemplating another five murders, and we've quickly got to establish the murderer's motives and reasoning."

D.C. Jane Morgan, added "A broken man speaks of avenge, not revenge. He wants atonement for a loved one and talks in the past tense as if she is no longer there. Did she advertise any personal services? If so did it result in her death or the loss of her love for this man? Why do five more people have to die? If he has to kill again why send the note risking detection? He either wants us to catch him unable to live with himself, or more likely with the threat of five more victims he feels superior and in control and thinks he can afford to tease us. If that's the case and he thinks we're struggling I wouldn't be surprised if he sent a further clue. If forensics do come up with something and we could sit on it for a while, not releasing it to the media, I think our inaction could frustrate him into sending us another clue."

"Or sending another body Jane" remarked one detective.

Jane Morgan had originally gained a degree and masters with distinctions in psychology and criminology and had joined the police force several years earlier and, under Arnold, was part of the team that had investigated three previous murders.

"Right!", the D.C.I. Snapped. "Until we have anything else to go on I want you to divide yourselves into two teams. One team will check up on everyone who advertised in the Evening Stars personal column's over the last two years using the A.B.C. method; accept nothing; believe nothing; challenge everything. That should go way past the time we need to look at. We require all names and addresses. The others will cover a fifty mile radius from Coventry city centre, establishing if any murders that took place could be connected to this kind of advertisement."

Dave Arnold received news about Tom Hopewell and was at his bedside an hour later holding a bag of grapes in one hand and a card in the other signed by all the team.

"Dave I'm not going to apologise. The only thing I'm sorry about was being found too soon."

"You haven't got anything to apologise for. I know how your wife's passing hit you hard. I can't even guess as to Lynn's." He passed the well wishing card across to Tom. "We're all there for you; all your friends down at the station. I'm just lost for words mate."

"Dave, because I've been saved doesn't make it any easier; if anything the pain inside is worse now than before. I know I can talk straight to you, and I feel sorry for all the surgeons hard work; not thanks, because I know that if I'm found too quick the next time, he'll try to do it all over again."

"Tom you've got to stop talking like that. You've got to live your life for Irene and Lynn. It's what they would have wanted."

"There's nothing here for me now and I know I'll try again. I won't be able to help myself."

"Okay Tom, I'll make you a deal. We've been friends a long time, joining the force around the same time and we both share the same principles on crime and punishment. For Lynn's sake stay positive; help us bring the bastard to justice. I'll keep you up to date on how the investigation's going and we'll both get him."

Arnold came away a while later, shaken by Tom's resolve and admittance that he would try again to kill himself, but by the very admission, it had allowed Dave to try to barter with Tom on Lynn's behalf, with a hope that it would buy time for him to think more clearly.

Jack looked again to Karina's picture on the mantlepiece, then switched his gaze to the porcelain statue on top of the bookshelf of Jesus upon the crucifix. "Forgive them Lord, for they know not what they do."

Jack was a great believer in fate and he had prayed many times each day for Karina when she was alive, begging forgiveness from God even though at that point he was a non-believer but his obsession demanded that prayers were said. His asking for absolution had continued daily after her death, knowing her sins were born of others targeting her vulnerability. The parasites gnawed away at Jacks mind, generating anger firstly, followed on by his depression. He battled within himself not to have the thoughts in the first place, which only made them enter his confused mind all the more.

CHAPTER EIGHT

An officer walked into the incident room. "The suspect, John Stamp has been arrested in Harrogate. A member of the public recognised the car from the news. He's being escorted down here as we speak."

An hour later Stamp was in the interview room accompanied by a duty solicitor. Arnold watched him from outside of the room via the remote viewing screen, letting him sweat. "He'll be exploding internally with anguish and uncertainty wanting us to get on with the questioning, not knowing exactly what we've got on him."

Stamp had the appearance of someone who hadn't exercised in years, his jumper too tight for his stomach that stretched over the belt that struggled to keep his trousers aloft; the double chins, appearing as if they were purposely developed just to support the face.

Arnold nodded twice to himself allowing a wry smile.

"The sweat should be running off him by now with his shape, cooped up in the small interview room" but Stamp sat still and remained calm which annoyed Arnold.

After the interview introduction was recorded, before D.S. Derek Smith Could ask a question, Stamp beat him to it. "Apparently it's been on the news saying that I could be of assistance to you, but I don't know how."

Arnold again watched him looking for any sign of nervousness. There was none.

"John, on four separate occasions last week your car was parked in the car park belonging to the Evening Star newspaper, where a woman who worked there was murdered on Friday. Why did you park there?"

He took no time in answering, no time to think. "I can assure you officer that cannot have been my car, perhaps one similar to it."

D.S. Smith showed him a photograph taken from the CCTV footage clearly outlining the registration, with an amazing likeness of himself at the wheel. Stamp sat in a rigid silence for several seconds as the solicitor looked towards him waiting for a reaction. Lines of bewilderment ran across Stamps brow. "I don't understand it. That appears to be my car, and also appears to be me but I can assure you it is not."

"Why would someone go to that extent of imitating you?"

"I can't understand it; what days was my car supposed to have been there?"

"Monday; Tuesday; Wednesday; Thursday. Ring any bells?"

"That's impossible. I was fishing on all those days. I do every week. I fish for hours, not coming away until around nine every night. Nobody could have taken my car during that time."

"Unless your twin's got a spare set of keys Mr. Stamp that's you at the steering wheel. You can't deny it. Okay then, although extremely doubtfully, let us assume it was someone else parked in the Evening Star car park, who were you fishing with that could swear you were there, when it is apparent that you weren't?"

"I fish there alone. That's why I go there. It's

so secluded; so peaceful." Stamp turned to the solicitor. "That isn't me in the photograph."

"John Stamp, I am terminating this interview and detaining you until such time as we have searched your house and forensics have finished with your car."

He was led away.

Jane Morgan who had been sitting in on the interview shook her head in amazement. " I can't believe there wasn't a single tell tale sign in his body language; he never lost his nerve for a second".

"We'll see how he holds up once we have the forensics." added D.S. Smith.

The following afternoon Stamp was re-interviewed. A sealed clear plastic bag was placed before him. "I am showing the suspect exhibit J.S. 1. Do you recognise the contents inside?"

"How the hell can I? It's folded up."

"Do you have a jumper of this colour?"

"Yes I do, but I don't know if that's it."

"John Stamp this jumper was removed from your house and hairs attached to it match the hair taken from you along with your saliva for DNA analysis--"

"Well they would do if it's my bloody jumper."

"Also on the jumper hairs were found that belonged to the murdered woman Lynn Tudor---"

"That's impossible I ---"

"Hairs from Lynn Tudor were also found inside your car. The tyre track found outside Tudor's cottage the day after her murder exactly matches that of the nearside tyre of your car, and also within the tread of the same tyre were traces of blood, which we believe, when the results come through will show the same DNA match to the dead hedgehog found in the mud imprinted by your tyre outside of the victim's cottage. What have you to say?"

"It can't be. It's impossible."

"Without waiting for the DNA results confirming both sets of blood are from the hedgehog, we have your car, with yourself at the wheel parked in the Evening Star car park wearing the jumper that Lynn Tudor's hair was found on. We have more than enough evidence against you." The interview was terminated. The Crown Prosecution Service were made aware of the whole proceedings, who then gave authorisation to charge him.

"John Stamp I charge you with the murder of Lynn Tudor, and anything you say will be taken down and used in evidence in a court of law."

"I've been framed! This isn't right! I've been fucking framed!"

Two officers had to drag Stamp away, screaming.

After completing the paperwork on the case, everyone went into the local pub for a celebratory drink which Dave Arnold paid for.

"Thank God we've got this nutter off the streets before he can kill anyone else" said D.C. Jim Dean.

Arnold agreed. "It went so smoothly and easily; I can't believe it. I wish every case was solved as quickly."

CHAPTER NINE

The following day Jack was sat at the breakfast table. He slammed his cup of tea down sending a cascade of searing liquid across the surface. "What do you mean? You've sent the police an untraceable clue. Who do you think you are? What kind of clue you idiot? Tell me what you've done."

"Jack I know everything you've planned has been with great care. I've watched the manner and thought you've given to every detail, even down to purchasing a mobile phone, trainers and clothing in one city one week that you would need, and the following week making the same purchases in another city and repeating this time and again. Different colours; different materials, all bought weeks ago, always thinking in advance not to leave the slightest connection of a clue. I have purchased several stencils with different sized lettering and various pencils and writing pads, none of them ever handled without gloves. The same too for the envelope which I posted well away from any CCTV cameras." said Ricky.

"I don't want your admiration. These are revenge attacks for my wife. I don't want to do this, I'm not really a murderer."

"You have murdered no-one, that's my job."

"Envelopes!!" shouted Jack. "What about hairs falling into them and your licking the envelopes and stamps. The police will have your DNA."

"Jack you're not listening, I've learnt from you. I wore a balaclava so no hairs could fall, and both the stamps and envelopes were self adhesive. Immediately after posting them I destroyed the stencil, pencil and writing pad."

"But you never mentioned a word when the papers said that a letter had been sent from the murderer and I accused some low life of trying to get in on the act for his own pathetic self importance."

Jack, as usual walked away. He needed time to think and went Into the back garden, immediately spotting the newly painted wording across the brickwork which repeated:

INDIGNATION. JUDGEMENT AWAITS

above the window, and

 THE OMNIPOTENT

below the window, once again with

SATAN

signed across the glass, which made him annoyed but realised he had greater needs to attend to. He couldn't afford to get too angry with Ricky. He couldn't kill anyone himself and went back into the lounge. Ricky was gone.

The team arrived in the morning ready to bring the enquiry paperwork up to date when another letter was received at the station addressed to Arnold, posted this time from Leicester. The envelope and note were bagged, the time recorded and rushed round to the Birmingham laboratory. A copy was quickly returned to the station and given across to the D.C.I. It was written in the same manner as the previous one, written with a different pencil, using a different sized stencil and with a note from the forensics lab explaining it was written on different paper.

JOHN WILL SAY NOTHING, THE ONE YOU HAVE CAUGHT.

UNTIL EACH ONE FOR THEIR SINS, JUSTICE IS BROUGHT.

I'LL POINT OUT THEIR TRANSGRESSIONS

UNTIL THEY LEARN WELL
SOME SOULS I'LL SAVE THOUGH OTHERS BURN IN HELL.   6-1

"Jesus! He's got a bloody accomplice. It's got to be for real, the code at the end is identical to the first letter; 6--1, which we assumed signified his intended victims" ranted Arnold. "What are we to make of the note? Jane have you any ideas?"

She nodded, still in thought. "Both letters have differing tones to them, possibly written by two people, but impossible to be certain. I think this second letter allows us to look into the mind of the very complex nature that surrounds the writer. By his words; each for their sins, justice is brought, Qisas."

"What does that mean?"

"It originates from Islamic teachings. An eye for an eye. I feel he also sees himself as a salvationist imposing redemption on his victims, although in his eyes he regards them as culpable which in his mind could make it acceptable in the eyes of his God. He feels no guilt in his actions and I find his religious overtones deeply disturbing. It could be that if we don't catch him by the time he has avenged his wife or girlfriend with his remaining intended five targets, he may then decide to save other lost souls and who knows where that would lead to."

Jack kept tuned in to all the news programmes at various times of the day when the local news came on the radio.

"Jesus! What have we started?" demanded Ricky. "Now her father's tried to kill himself."

"I've told you before, he could have saved her if only he'd been a good parent and pointed out the errors of her ways."

"But Jack the guy's innocent, and what about the families of your other targets. Will they all be guilty too?"

"What! A drug dealer? Do you think he comes

from a stable caring background. His parents are more guilty than he is. They shaped his future. Karina was baited until she became totally dependant on the drugs before the dealer gave her to the pimp so that she'd need more drugs. Do you think she was the first he'd done it to?, and what about me? I'm a victim of their abuse of Karina; don't I count?"

Ricky never responded.

CHAPTER TEN

Joe Holland was a loud, repulsive excuse of a man; slim built, and small, yet capable of creating dread in his unfortunate neighbours living in the same block of four flats that Holland occupied in Coventry. A continuous flow of noisy, troublesome individuals visited Holland's flat at all hours of the night, in search of their much needed fix. It eventually led to one neighbour through despair, calling the police, who raided his flat. Unfortunately it was one of the rare occasions that Holland had no drugs on the premises.

Within minutes of the police calling off their search, he ran amok, brandishing a baseball bat, slamming it into the walls, screaming for all to hear, that if the police ever came back he would set fire to the whole block of flats, even though he had no proof if it was a neighbour who had called them in.

Holland was regularly high to the

point of near unconsciousness and often addicts who came calling after three in the morning were sometimes unable to get a response from him, shouting loudly up to his flat through desperation.

Years earlier Holland had dealt drugs in Birmingham and used to supply both Jack and Karina when they both lived there, before Jack knew her. Holland had operated for several years in Coventry, though not seeing Jack for a long time had sold him five wraps of heroin the day before without recognising him.

With Holland's vacant look, Jack doubted he'd even remember his own mother.

Karina had told Jack when they first met of how the dealer had initially befriended her before introducing her to his world of drugs. He had gradually got Karina taking heroin before making her completely dependant upon it, later introducing her to a friend of his who was a pimp. She was like putty in their hands. Holland's time had come.

Around nine pm, waiting in the shadows, in the quiet cul de sac, confident he was not seen, Ricky rang his doorbell, once again dressed in his overalls and balaclava. He rang repeatedly for five minutes until an agitated slurring voice over the intercom shouted "Piss off."

"I've brought the eighty pounds I owe you."

After a lengthy silence the reply came. "Bring it tomorrow."

"I can't, I'm leaving town tonight."

In his drug induced state, money was still the driving force, whoever's money. He pressed the door release allowing Ricky to enter. Holland lived on the first floor and after hurriedly climbing the stairs to avoid being seen by anyone in his balaclava, Ricky knocked on his door. No-one came. He tried the handle and was amazed when it opened.

"A drug dealer with an open door, he must be well out of it."

When he saw Holland lying on the settee in a trance like state Ricky couldn't believe he had even managed the simple task of pressing the security button to allow him entry. He looked around the room and saw an enormous expensive television screen, the whole flat adorned with quality furnishings; the trappings of a drug dealer.

"You have led Karina's downfall and Jack is right to make you pay." He muttered to himself.

He took five syringes from a pouch and walked over to Holland where he wrapped a tourniquet around his arm until a vein stood proud whereupon he slowly inserted the first syringe pushing the liquid through until the chamber was empty. "That's right, you lie there while I give you all your heroin back. You are definitely going to be the easiest one to deal with." He did the same again, inserted the needle and after the cylinder emptied he left it hanging out of his arm, resting on a cushion, the same as the first. Holland could only blink in slow motion, occasionally opening his mouth to speak but no sound coming out, his blank stare uncaring, doubtful he even knew what was happening to him. The remaining syringes were emptied, one after the other, into his veins in both arms, the empty needles protruding from them. Ricky took his picture on another new mobile phone.

He let himself out dropping the latch behind him not wanting Holland to be discovered for a while, doubtful that if anyone did, they could save him.

Back at the car, parked down the dark cul de sac, Ricky went through the rigorous undressing procedure to eliminate the possibility of leaving the slightest clue behind. Once again Jack would destroy all that he wore and the following morning he would have his tyres changed, again at different garages in a different town before sending the photo of Holland through to the police. Jack knew they would be unable to piece anything together as neither Karina or himself had bought drugs off him for many years.

CHAPTER ELEVEN

Late the following morning Arnold received a photograph on his mobile, showing Holland with the syringes hanging from his arms, unaware of who the victim was. The code followed on in text; 6--2, indicating that it was the second intended murder of six. The police hadn't divulged the original contents of the note to the media.

"How the hell did the murderer get my number" Arnold blurted out. He immediately checked with the network, but they couldn't confirm the sender of the text and the phone signal was dead.

Arnold took it through to the inquiry room.

D.S. Derek Smith spoke up. "I know a few of us have two mobiles; one for personal use and the other one, to receive tip offs from Informants, journalists etc. I wonder if Lynn Tudor could possibly have had one of your cards which the murderer might have stolen, or even if one of her father's cards had your number on?"

"Doubtful" mumbled Arnold, "but not impossible."

The image was checked against police files though failed to bring up a name, so the media were asked to carry the picture in an attempt to discover the victim's identity. After the evening news had been broadcast they received calls within minutes pinpointing both the victim and his address.

It was established that Holland had been killed by a massive drugs overdose but the police were surprised to find that there was no forced entry leading them to think that he could have known his killer.

The forensic team was at the murder scene all day. Again everyone in the immediate vicinity were questioned, without anyone hearing or seeing any thing suspicious. Holland's computer was taken by the police along with his mobile phone and several notebooks bearing many names.

Dave Arnold made a televised appeal for anyone with information to come forward, emphasising that although a man had been charged with the murder of Lynn Tudor, his unknown accomplice could be involved with the murder of Joe Holland.

The following day an elderly man walked into Coventry Central station to say he'd seen something out of the ordinary on the night of the murder. Dave Arnold was introduced to him. "What exactly did you see mister Richards?"

"When I went to my daughters it was dark. There's a short cut I take down a mostly disused alley and round by several derelict garages. It's a quiet place. I noticed a red Fiat parked there with its rear windows blacked out. When I was returning there was a man stood outside the car apparently muttering to himself or someone out of view behind the tinted glass. The one remaining street light in the road at the other side of the garages only just made the alley area visible. I stopped and waited in the shadows because the man acted in a strange manner."

"What time would this have been?"

"Around nine thirty."

"How do you mean he was acting strangely?"

"Well apart from his mumbling, he wore a

balaclava and he started to undress outside of the car. He took a bin liner from the car and then removed his balaclava, overalls, shirt and trousers which he placed into the bin liner. He took off a pair of gloves that he was wearing, also placing them in the liner, but lastly, oddly, stood right next to the car and stepped out of his shoes and into the Fiat barefoot. At least I don't think he had socks on but as I said there wasn't much light. He then hung a carrier bag outside the car while he put his shoes in and placed that into the bin liner which he placed into a second liner before driving off."

"Did you notice which model of Fiat it was?"

"Yes it was a Punto but an old one."

"I don't suppose you caught the registration?"

"I couldn't see it at all?"

"Would you recognise him again?"

"No, I couldn't see his face in the semi-darkness and most of the time his back was turned towards me."

"Could you make out anything that he was muttering?"

"Nothing at all, only that whatever he said, he

said in an angry growling tone."

"Could you see anyone else in the car?"

" I couldn't see if anyone was in the back because of the windows, nor the front because from where I was stood, the back of the car was facing me."

"Did you notice anyone in the car when you first passed, walking by the front of the car."

"There was no one in either the front or the back as I could clearly see through the front windscreen, peering in through curiosity because of where it was parked, unless they were crouched down in the back behind the seat which would have made it impossible for me to see."

"Could you see the colours of his clothing?"

"Not at all, only that they were dark rather than light."

"What about the colour of his shoes?"

"I'm not even certain they were shoes, I just assumed they were. I'm sorry I don't seem to have been of much help."

"Mr Richards your help is invaluable. I would like you to take us to the alley where the car was parked and if you can remember any other detail along the way regardless of how small, it could be of the greatest importance."

The area was sealed off and forensics brought in and a footprint was discovered appearing to be from a trainer, and a tyre tread mark was found close by the footprint.

The twentieth of November in the Witton cemetery, Birmingham.

Jack had thrown the long-dead flowers into the nearby waste bin and carefully replaced them with a dozen red roses. As he knelt to position the flowers he looked up to the gravestone before him and touched it, apologising to Karina for not visiting her since September. "I have so much to do in your name, so much planning and detail; and then, when all is taken care of, I will be back with you." He placed a kiss onto his fingers before pressing them gently onto her engraved name.

The twenty first of November in the Friends of Layton cemetery, Blackpool.

Gregor Natas removed the withered flowers and replaced them with the new blooms he had bought outside of the cemetery gates. The date appeared before him on the headstone. "James it's nearly ten years since you left us. I am still upset and angry at how you were taken from us and I cannot find peace. That will only happen when I'm back with you." said Gregor quietly, in his Eastern European accent.

CHAPTER TWELVE

The following day another letter was received addressed to D. C. I. Arnold. The envelope was again rushed across to the Birmingham laboratory, where, a short while later, a copy of the note was returned back to them and as with the first two, a great deal of care had been taken not to provide any clue. It appeared to be drawn up in exactly the same manner as the previous ones, again using a different size stencil, with the laboratory stating that it was made up from a different paper and pencil to the first two. It read:

THE EVIL THIS DEMON TRADED IN

TURNED HER NAIVETY INTO SIN

AND UNABLE TO TURN BACK AGAIN

WAS FORCED TO PURCHASE FROM DOWN THE LANE

BUT FOR HIS PART IN RUINING MY WIFE

REGRETTABLY, I'VE SAVED HIS NEXT LIFE. 6-2.

The copied letter was pinned to the white board where everyone viewed it before they collectively attempted to decipher its significance. "From the first part it appears that the murderer's wife was introduced to drugs and became hooked on them though I don't get the part about the lane." said D.I. Sarah Brown.

"Is there any lane on record that is used above others, from a dealer's point of view?" added Derek Smith. The D.C.I. suggested a different line of thought. "Perhaps her need was a greater one than she could afford. She was possibly driven down a lane used by prostitutes. That could be why he referred to his wife being ruined and turning to sin. Have you any ideas on the letter Jane?"

"Talk of demons and evil but most importantly he repeats saving his victim again for the next life by killing him in this one strengthening my belief that he sees himself as a Salvationist. He must be caught. Is there any way we can put additional pressure on John Stamp to cooperate?"

D.S. Smith re-interviewed Stamp. " Look John two people have now been murdered. You are not responsible for the second murder and it's quite possible that you had no physical involvement with the death of Lynn Tudor." Smith purposely said nothing further, expecting a quick response from Stamp, who remained silent. "If that is the case being an accomplice would drastically reduce any prison term. If you cooperate and give me the name of the murderer the judge would be made aware that your cooperation possibly saved the lives of the other victims." Smith stopped again assuming Stamp would want to talk, especially being falsely offered a possible way out. Again he said nothing.

"John are you a religious man?"

He stayed quiet. The D.S. turned to his solicitor.

"Mr. Thomas, Have you advised your client to remain silent? It would certainly be in his best interest to assist us."

"Why should I speak? You've charged me with murder. However those pictures of my car with me inside in the Evening Star car park were obtained; and my front tyre tracks at her cottage, the dead hedgehog and hairs found from the victim, what chance have I got? All that I can say is to repeat what I have said all along, that somebody has gone to great lengths to frame me. One thing that did come to mind, I had to replace two registration plates within two weeks that had gone missing, thinking they had fallen off. Who loses two plates within a fortnight? nobody. They were obviously stolen to use on another car to make it look like mine. I can give you the name of the shop that made the new ones. I've no enemies. I haven't a clue what's happened but you won't believe a word of it. If I'm truthful, and I was sat where you are with the so called evidence to hand, I'd feel exactly the same as you do, only I'm innocent and can't help you because I know nothing and I, as much as you, want you to catch the bastard responsible because until you do, no jury in this country will find me innocent."

"There's no point in taking the questioning any further. Be it on your head if anyone else is murdered." said the D.S. before terminating the interview.

Back in the incident room discussing the way to go forward with the investigation D.S. Derek Smith spoke out. "Let's look at who else might be his possible targets. He's killed Lynn Tudor, a totally innocent victim who was unfortunate enough to be in charge of the personal ad's column. He's now murdered a drug dealer. The killer has another four victims lined up and I wonder if they are in order as to how he considered they contributed to his wife's downfall. If that were to be the case, who would be next? After her addiction we think she may have turned to prostitution and if so did she have a pimp?"

The D.C.I. agreed with Derek. "We can't take any chances. A team of detectives will work the red light district tonight in Coventry city centre looking out for a red Punto and asking the prostitutes if they knew of, or used the dealer. Also find out if they know of any other working girl who could have used the dealer, or any pimp, without letting the pimps know. Make it clear to them that if any pimps knew him they could be a possible target. If any do know him we'll have to observe their patches without them being aware."

D.C. Kate Jones was driving close to where Holland lived, when she noticed a red Fiat Punto with darkened rear windows parked down an alley, as if to keep it out of sight as there were many parking spaces on the street. The car registration was checked and belonged to an Ivan Jovanovic.

He was brought in for questioning while forensics scrutinised his car.

He sat opposite D.I. Sarah Brown and D.C. Morgan. He had dark hair with a high receding line.

"Mr. Jovanovic are you married?"

He nodded."She left me four years ago."

"Do you know your wife's whereabouts now?"

"No."

"You drive a red Fiat Punto, is that correct?"

"I bought it a year ago. Is that what this is all about?"

"Where were you on the fifth of November in the car?"

"I was out of the country."

"Where were you on the tenth of November?"

" I went back to my country to visit my family. I was there from mid October only arriving back two days ago. I can show you the documentation and my passport which has been stamped."

Once they had been produced and nothing was found on the Fiat, Jovanovic was released.

The night was damp and cold as D.S. Derek Smith walked through Butcher Lane alone, few lights illuminating the area. He felt uncomfortable, although his colleague was in view further down the lane on the other side. He was quickly approached by one of several women lining the road edge.

"Are you looking for a good time?"

He was surprised by her good looks. *What is she doing down here*? his thoughts, until his mind quickly cleared; *same as all the rest. Drugs I should imagine.*

"What's your name?" he asked.

"Mandy. What was you looking for?"

"Mandy, I'm sorry but I'm not down here for that." He took out his identification, which forced her back a step.

"Jesus! Don't say you're busting me. I've only just started my shift." she said in desperation, panicking that tomorrows fix would no longer be affordable.

"Relax. I'm not interested in what you do, but I am here to protect you."

"What do I need your fucking protection for? Oh! I get it, some kind of freebie. You can forget it."

"Mandy listen. Have you heard about a dealer called Joe Holland being murdered?"

She stood in silence.

"Did you know him?"

"I knew of him." she replied.

"We need to know of any pimps that used him for drugs, as they may be in danger."

"Is that what he got killed for, selling dodgy gear?"

"No, but any pimp who bought from him

could be in danger."

Mandy stared at him as she took out her mobile and rang a friend to explain what she'd been told. She described the sergeant and finished the conversation.

"Must be something big. Apparently there's at least four more of you guys asking the same questions all over the lane. You can't really expect anyone to come and tell you they're a pimp."

"Not even if their life could be in danger?"

"Jesus! they really are a target too?"

"Mandy we need to know who used Holland."

"The word is a few pimps are running scared, but they still won't come forward; more frightened of you lot."

D.S. Smith shifted tack, lying. "The girls under their control could also be in danger."

Mandy used her phone again to ring three different friends and when she finished the calls she gave the sergeant three girls names and told him which patch they would be on. "Be quiet when you talk to them. They daren't let their pimps know their names have been given. All the girls are scared over Holland's murder so if you are staking their patches out, for Pete's sake don't let the pimps cotton on or they'll put two and two together and the girls will really get it."

After discreetly talking to the prostitutes it was established that four of the pimps in the area had purchased drugs from Holland, and from the girls descriptions they were soon pinpointed and observed from a distance.

"Three o'clock in the bloody morning and no single approach made to any pimp, no suspicious vehicles or anyone loitering other than the sad bastards who are having to pay for it."

"Never mind Derek", said Sarah. "Only another hour to go then that's us finished."

"Maybe, but it's the same again tomorrow and until the killer's caught."

At three thirty the lane was deserted and two of the pimps with their girls walked away, followed at a safe distance by plain clothes police officers in pairs. The other pimps picked up by taxis, were followed by unmarked cars. Once they arrived at their homes, the police were relieved by colleagues who stayed all night, watching the premises.

Halfway through the third night of keeping watch on the lane, Sarah poked Derek in the ribs to get his attention, resting with closed eyes, his seat slightly reclined. He sat up sharply. "What's up?"

"Over there. A Punto with blacked out windows. It could be red; not easy to make out its exact colour in this light." Sarah got on the radio as her colleague drove slowly towards the Punto, causing the prostitute, who was bent over, talking through the window, to stand upright angrily muttering to herself.

"What bleeding chance have I got with them around?"

"What's up?" asked the punter.

Realising immediately that she'd made a mistake, she tried to think of a reply so he wouldn't become wary and disappear on her. Too late with her response, he spotted the slow moving vehicle. "Bitch!!" he shouted, before screeching off at speed.

Keeping their position clear over the

radio, two other patrol cars joined the chase, lights flashing, but the Punto only gathered more speed, mounting the kerb at one street corner, demolishing a section of fencing before it was manoeuvred back onto the road heavily scraping along two parked cars until the driver lost control altogether hitting a lamp-post, and coming to a complete stop. Seconds later, having gathered his senses, the driver scrambled out to run; straight into the arms of D.S. Smith who bundled him to the ground, assisted by another officer. Within minutes he was in the back of a police van on his way to the station.

Arnold was informed, and twenty minutes later was being briefed at his office. The only words that the suspect had uttered was to demand a solicitor. The suspect was in his late twenties, scruffily dressed, emitting an aroma reminiscent of someone living amongst several dogs.

In the interview room the proceedings got underway. "I am D.S. Scott Andrews. With me in the interview room is D.S. Kate Jones. For the benefit of the tape would you give your name and address?"

The suspect shook his head and Andrews looked to the duty solicitor. "Mr. Jeffries, although it is his right to remain silent, I think you should advise your client to co-operate. What is it that he has to hide?"

Jeffries looked towards his client who resolutely once again shook his head. Arnold again watched from outside the room and although frustrated at the suspects silence felt a surge of adrenalin because of his silence, convinced they had their second killer.

"For the benefit of the tape the interviewee refuses to speak. At approximately eleven thirty on the twenty fourth of November, you were requested to stop your vehicle, but drove off at speed. Why was that?" After a few seconds silence D.S. Andrews continued.   "For the sake of the tape, the suspect still refuses to speak. Two further vehicles joined in the chase to apprehend you but you continued to drive away erratically at high speed in an attempt to evade them. The Fiat Punto you drove is registered as owned by a Mr. Fry who we have spoken to. He apparently sold the vehicle, the new owner promising to send all relevant documentation to the D.V.L.A.

A Fiat Punto fitting the description of the one you were driving is connected to a murder. Due to our enquiries it was expected that the killer would next visit Coventry's red light district, his next victim, most probably a pimp-----"

"Hang on a minute" interrupted the suspect. "You can't pin that on me. I thought you were chasing me because the car isn't taxed or insured. I'll give you whatever information you want. I'm no murderer."

"What is your name and address?"

" Jack Green. I live at seven Ivory Villa's in Leicester."

In the adjoining room Green's criminal file was brought up and handed to D.S. Jones during the interview.

"Are you the owner of a dark orange Fiat Punto, registration W 859 TLF"

"Yes I bought it about six months ago and I must have forgotten to post the paperwork off."

"If you live in Leicester, why drive to Coventry to visit the red light district."

"I was through visiting friends and before I went back I wanted sex; simple as that."

"I'll require their names and addresses. My officer's have told me you negotiated the minor roads in your attempt to escape with an obvious knowledge of the area. Is that correct?"

"I lived in Coventry until seven years ago. I used to deliver for a catalogue company so I know it like the back of my hand."

"Do you know Wilby Lane like the back of your hand?"

"I've never heard of it."

"I can see on your file that you were imprisoned for G.B.H. Handy with your fists are you?"

Green remained silent.

"According to the records, shortly after your release you spent time in a mental health unit after trying to kill yourself."

"Here we go. I wondered what this was all about." He looked to his solicitor. " They are after stitching me up. I haven't done anything wrong. I should never have been sent down for so long. Anyone should have the right to defend their wife's integrity."

In the adjoining room, outwardly, Arnolds appearance never faltered. Inwardly the surge of adrenalin ran again. Jack Green spoke in the same manner that the notes were written in!

"What was said or done to your wife for you to lose your temper in this way?"

"Why are you bringing the past up?" said Green. "I thought I was answering questions on the present."

"You serve time for standing up for your wife and then visit a prostitute for sex before you go home to her------"

"My wife died over three years ago in a road accident screamed Green, his nose flaring; hatred briefly burning in his cold stare towards D.S. Andrews.

"You look as if you would like to kill me. That temper of yours is a real problem. Where were you on the evening of the fifth of November?"

"How the hell should I know. That's ages ago."

"Where were you on the fifteenth of November?"

" I remember that night because it was my

mother's birthday when she was alive. I was at home alone."

"Convenient."

Green's stare was intense towards the D.S., the hatred a little more controlled.

"I'm going to bring this interview to a close so I can study your file more closely, meanwhile you will be held in custody while your home is searched and your car subjected to forensics."

Green glanced across to his solicitor, who reminded the D.S. On how long he could hold his client for without charge.

There was no need for a DNA sample as it was already on the data-base, and while Green's record was checked a search got underway on his house, a two bedroom semi-detached property in a sought after area of Leicester. Although it had been purchased as a first time buy, jointly by Jack Green and his wife, the mortgage had been fully repaid within five years, prior to his wife's death. There was also a second house recorded in Coventry as owned by Green. Arnold checked his employment details which revealed his low inconsistent income would struggle to meet the ordinary monthly mortgage repayments on the cheapest house. After bringing his wife's details up, it was immediately apparent how the home had been quickly repaid and another one purchased; She had been before the court on two separate occasions, under the same offence; she was a prostitute. "It's slowly coming together" Arnold whispered to himself.

"He's the second killer."

At Green's home, the place was stripped bare; most floorboards lifted while a camera was inserted below to closely examine every nook and cranny, especially after discovering in his study, a desk containing many books on serial killers. After the search was finalised his computer was taken away for analysis. His second property in Coventry was visited and after meeting with the letting agents was found to be up for rent or sale without any interest or tenant for over six months. His mobile phone history was investigated without anything un-towards emerging from a call point, until the names on his library were checked. Joe Holland's name and number was among them. D.S. Kate Jones rang Arnold. "Bob Jacobs, one of Jack Green's buddies went down for six months for aiding and abetting him in the attack for which Green was jailed; seems they planned it together, and Holland's number's in there too."

"Good work Kate. We're halfway to nailing him. I'll organise Jacob's house to be searched while we bring him in for questioning. I also want you to contact Mr. Richards who witnessed the Fiat Punto parked at the garages. Find out the exact time he first saw the car, because in his statement he said it was dark. I'll arrange for Green's car to be at the garages tonight and I want Richards there at the same precise time to see if it could be possible in the dim light to be mistaken about the shade of the car colouring, as there's not a massive difference."

Jacobs was brought in for questioning while his house was searched without anything suspicious being found. The interview was terminated when his alibi's were substantiated.

Later that night after Richards had stated that it might possibly have been the car he saw, Jack Green was reinterviewed.

"You said that you couldn't recall your whereabouts on the evening of the fifth of

November. You also declared that you'd never heard of Wilby Lane. I put it to you that on the evening in question you were down Wilby Lane with your accomplice John Stamp."

Green screamed back "I don't know of any damn lane by that name. Nor do I know of any John Stamp".

"You're losing it again. Did you lose it when you slashed Tudor's throat, or was that Stamps doing?"

He never replied, as he looked towards the ceiling.

"Did you lend your car to anyone?"

"I don't lend anyone my car." he said in a more controlled manner.

"What about Bob Jacobs?"

"What the hell's he got to do with all of this?"

"Don't act so surprised. He's been to prison once for helping you attempt to kill your last victim."

"I've never attempted to kill anyone. I've already told you, he spread lies about my wife, and I just wanted to teach him a lesson."

"What lies did your victim mention? The fact

that your wife was a prostitute; that would have been no lie. That's what she was."

Green was exploding inside, trying hard to keep it in. He rubbed his right hand over and over his head. God how he wanted to punch the D.S., and as though his solicitor detected his edginess he asked the inspector for a break so that he could speak to his client.

D.S.Andrews knew his brief had intervened to give Green breathing space to calm down.

"No Mr. Jeffries! -- Must be tight making ends meet now the bread winner's gone. After all she repaid the mortgage in record time due to her activities---------"

"We both paid the house off. We both worked."

"Who are you trying to fool? You were in and out of work and when you were working, it was for peanuts; then there's your second house that you still have a mortgage on that can't attract a tenant or a buyer, and you're threatened with repossession. No Mr. Green, I think you were pissed off when your wife died and it left you struggling desperately for cash; unable to find a buyer for the house, even though It's been on the market for over two years. I feel her demise and your resulting predicament worked your quick anger up to such a degree that you decided to kill those you felt were responsible for your wife turning to prostitution in the first place. The notes you sent us spell it all out."

" I've sent no notes; I've been down no lane; I've killed no-one. Yes I've been down for grievous bodily harm, and in the absence of anyone else to blame you're fitting me up."

"We don't fit people up. We find the evidence to convict them and most give themselves away by their own stupidity. One; a witness saw a Fiat Punto, his description matching your car, parked close to the scene of the second murder, the car's occupant obviously involved by what the witness observed. Two; you have Holland's mobile number in your phone library and he had dealings with both yourself and your wife when she was alive. It's highly likely that he was your intended target when you went to jail -------"

" D.S. Andrews as you quite rightly pointed out, my client went to prison for assaulting someone, other than Holland; you cannot assume his target was Holland because it fits conveniently into your murder inquiry."

"He was stopped with a hammer in his hand at Holland's front door by a neighbour who he hit several times with the instrument leading to his jail sentence. I put it to you that your intended target was Joe Holland."

"Yes I knew him. I bought drugs off him but it was only coincidence that I was near his door. I never knew where he lived, as he only dealt from a corner on a side street not too far away".

"Then why was you in the vicinity brandishing a hammer?"

Green never replied.

" I repeat where were you on the fifteenth of November being the night that Joe Holland was murdered with a heroin overdose, found with five emptied syringes hanging out of his veins?"

" You cannot pin that on me!"

The officer stared at Green saying nothing, only watching him squirming uncomfortably in his chair.

The D.S. switched his gaze from the suspect

to the solicitor and quickly back again. "Three; the killer from his notes to us is known to be avenging his dead wife by murdering the people he holds responsible for her being a prostitute. Four; it was our belief that the next intended victim would be from the red light area. Low and behold, you arrive, only to flee the police when they try to detain you. Five; a search of your house has turned up your morbid fascination with serial killers. Jack Green it is my belief that together with John Stamp you both contrived to kill six people, two of whom are already dead. At this stage I shall not be charging you but I will apply to the court to further detain you while investigations continue."

The interview was terminated and Jack Green was taken away, protesting his innocence.

Both Arnold and D.S. Andrews discussed the case. "If the footprint from the murder scene hadn't been a size smaller than Green's feet and if the tyre tread on his car had matched the imprint at the garages, I think the C.P.S. would have allowed us to charge him. Those two elements alone would cast doubt of his guilt by a jury. Everything we have is circumstantial. We need something concrete."

After holding Green for as long as possible, without any evidence being discovered by forensics, Arnold reluctantly had to release him.

CHAPTER THIRTEEN

Gregor Natas sat next to his lounge window as the rain bounced off it. He neither heard nor saw it, staring into space. He didn't need to concentrate to be back there; it was as if it had happened yesterday albeit years earlier. The words flooded back to him.

"Donald Stamford, you are charged with manslaughter, that while under the influence of alcohol and without holding a driving licence or insurance, you drove a car, registration L586 GRP, knocking James Durakovic from his cycle, killing him instantly. How do you plead?"

"Not guilty."

Stamford, with alcohol in his system, although beneath the legal limit, tried in a convincing manner to sway the jury into believing that James had somehow lost his balance and swerved wildly into the path of the car leaving no chance of avoiding hitting him. He apologised for the death of James explaining that he had nightmares every night, crying himself to sleep regularly.

"Liar! Liar!" Gregor had shouted in his Eastern European accent, and was duly warned by the judge. He remembered the uncaring look in Stamford's eyes as he had stared at James' lifeless body, before the look was replaced by fear; frightened for his own skin. He stared directly at the jurors saying he couldn't imagine what James' mother was going through as he himself had six year old twin sons. That was the reason he had driven the car that morning, taking one of his boys to the local accident and emergency unit at the hospital after he had injured his ankle and was unable to contact the boy's mother.

The prosecution asked why he hadn't rung for a taxi, to which he replied that he had, calling two taxi offices and was told every office was busy due to the heavy traffic, being a Saturday morning and he would have to wait up to an hour. When asked by the prosecution which were those taxi offices, Stamford replied that he couldn't remember, getting them from the telephone directory while in a state of panic.

Stamford's solicitor argued, that although his client had a legal amount of alcohol in his system, the deceased had a greater amount in his, and was sixteen years of age. He added that both cyclists had been drinking on the day of the accident whereas his client had only consumed a minimum amount the night before, making the witness' statement for the prosecution unreliable, especially in view of the fact that both were related, feeling a need to direct blame at someone for the loss of his cousin and friend.

The jury retired to deliberate and reached a unanimous decision. They returned a guilty verdict. The Judge said he sympathised with Stamford in one sense for urgently needing to get his injured son to the hospital for treatment, but that he should have rung an ambulance, unable to legally drive with the result of someone losing their life. He then passed sentence of two years but only served eighteen months.

Gregor Natas was at his Aunt Julies house, comforting her as best he could, never able to come to terms with losing James at sixteen years old. Julie had been a bubbly socialite, always the first name on many guest lists of forthcoming events. She was bright, sharp and witty where people would gather around her to hear the latest comical tale, never knowing if it was true or not; not really caring as each one fascinated and entertained. Since James' death she had become a different person, unrecognisable, never going out if she could avoid it and Gregor was never sure upon turning up if his aunt would let him in, her door unanswered on many occasions when he knew she was at home, but as he arrived she was stood in the garden throwing bread to the birds. The day was sunny but she was wrapped up against the cold. They both walked into the house.

"Julie I had to see you today of all days; ten years since James died and I wanted to be with you."

Gregor passed his aunt a tissue as a tear rolled away, her eyes red, her distraught face belying her age.

"It doesn't seem so long ago that you were both out riding your bicycles. His killer will be getting on with his life now, doubtful if he will have any idea of what today actually is. I remember he had six year old twin sons; a fact his solicitor brought up to attempt to get sympathy from the Judge. His sons will be sixteen now, the same age as when James died."

Gregor took a note book from the cabinet that contained the names and addresses of the Judge, solicitor and driver who had killed James. "No insurance! No MOT! No driving licence even. He shouldn't have been on the road, but to have driven in drink in my eyes makes him a murderer. Eighteen months! Only eighteen months and then okay to get back on with the rest of his life.

CHAPTER FOURTEEN

Shaun Dixon was an evil human being, feared by other pimps, enough to stay away from his patch,encouraged by the unsolved disappearance of others who dared try to muscle in on his territory. He controlled six prostitutes, working in pairs. He would personally escort two out to their ground, swapping for another pair the following evening. None would dare to rip him off. One woman who tried had her face slashed too terrified to report him to the police. He was six foot tall, with a muscular body; a requirement he felt was needed in his profession to warn off would-be troublemakers.

Jack waited patiently down the dark alleyway. Dixon eventually walked into view around eight p.m. with a young woman either side of him. One of the women stopped at the edge of a disused shop's doorway while the other two walked on. A hundred metres further down the road the other woman stopped and pulled her skirt up close to her thigh and stepped out to the edge of the pavement. The pimp moved back between the two women and retreated into the shadows.

Throughout the night, car after car pulled up to the women with their windows wound down, and after talking with them, either drove off alone or with one of the prostitutes. Occasionally Dixon would go to them on their return and take money from them until three in the morning when a taxi pulled up and all three climbed in. Jack followed. The women were dropped off together, Dixon taken home. His house, detached, in an expensive area of Birmingham made Jack realise how the women afforded him a grand life style while they were allowed to keep little more than their much needed drug money, as he recalled it as Karina had described during her earlier years. Jack knew the prostitute's needs would have them ready to be back on the streets again the following evening, to earn their much needed fix.

He parked further down the road from Dixon's house but was slightly concerned that there was nowhere to be totally out of view from neighbouring houses while he observed the pimps house. He needed to keep parking in different places over the following nights remaining inconspicuous while he watched who came and went. He needed Ricky to be certain of having the pimp alone to administer his punishment undisturbed.

Each night at seven thirty Dixon left by taxi to pick up the prostitutes ready for their night's work.

At six thirty, in the darkness, Ricky rang his doorbell with the car parked out of sight several streets away.

Dixon opened the door, immediately tasered, and fell backwards stunned and temporarily incapacitated, before Ricky administered chloroform and prepared him for his awakening.

He came around and attempted to scream, the strong tape across his mouth preventing him from doing so, forcing the air through his nostrils as if driven by bellows, the agony unbearable. His mind was a disorientated fog as the effect of the chloroform left him. He quickly learnt to keep perfectly still as any movement forced searing pain throughout his body. His arms were spread reaching into both top corners of the door frame, held firmly in position, by strong nails, driven through both hands as though upon a crucifix. His feet were capable of touching the floor if he stood on his tiptoes, but were incapable of kicking out by ropes round his ankles attached to the bottom corners of the door frame allowing the minimum of movement. His weight had been taken up by a rope affixed to the top of the door frame and wrapped tightly around his waist before being hoisted up. The mist gradually cleared from him and so Ricky let the rope slacken that took his weight. His wide frightened eyes asked the question that his mouth was unable to do."Why?"

Ricky wanted more. He would not talk yet, only stare, allowing the extreme fear to become sheer terror letting Dixon know, see and feel the total hopelessness of his situation. Just as the women felt.

Eventually Ricky spoke without shifting his gaze. Dixon's eyes also remained firmly fixed, frightened to lose eye contact, scared of any unknown punishment for doing so.

"In one minute I will remove the tape so that you may speak. If you shout out there is no-one that can hear you and it will be replaced immediately. You are to die here today. It is your choice of how. There is no way to change your fate. If you plead for your life, the choices will be cancelled and you will die in unbelievable agony. Say nothing other than that which I order you to say and you will have a painless release into the next life. I want to hear repeatedly, your denunciation of God. You are not to beg for forgiveness or exclaim regret, for in the Lords eyes he may let you back in. Of the six people it is my duty to deliver from this life, your vile existence will not allow my friend to attempt to save your evil soul. I will now remove the tape but speak any word other than that which you are prompted and it will result in a long agonising death. You are here to pay the price for the women you have debased but more especially for one in particular whose name I shall not mention, Do you understand the terms for removing the tape?"

Dixon nervously nodded his head.

"After I remove your gag you are to repeat the words I read out to you but I warn you not to utter any other word." Ricky selected the video mode on the new mobile phone and then ripped the tape from the pimps mouth causing a deep sigh of relief, although almost immediately his taut senses returned to his dire situation. "I don't know who the fuck you are, but you better let me down now----".Before he could scream out another word, he was knocked senseless once again by the tazer.

When he came to, the tape had been replaced over his mouth. Dixon strained with all his might to free his hands from the nails, his face twisted with indescribable pain, his efforts futile because of the large washers that had been placed under the head of the nails holding him secure. He grimaced in agony as the blood poured from his palms. Ricky opened a briefcase at his side and, as Dixon watched, he brought out a hammer, a large carving knife, a saltcellar and a small plastic container where liquid splashed against the inside.

"If you try that again, I'll crush all of your

toes!!!" Ricky screamed as he violently swung the hammer at the desk, completely dislodging the corner. Ricky calmed himself. "I will remove your tape once again and pour a drink for you which you will swallow completely. If it is not drunk I will replace the tape to quell the attempted screaming as I cut open your arms, legs and stomach of which salt will be poured into their wounds. This will only intensify the pain you feel as you writhe in vain to be free from the nails. This will not kill you. Neither will your toes crushed beneath my hammer. Your slow death will arrive from the blood that drains away from the slits in your wrists as the battery acid I pour into your eyes makes certain of a long excruciating exit from this, your irreligious existence. Do you understand?"

Dixon half nodded.

Ricky removed the tape and told him what to say. "I have no God, there is no God. I do not seek forgiveness for my sins."

After needing prompting again Dixon repeated the words and the mobile was paused as his next lines were read out which he again repeated fearfully. "I have led a wicked life, preying on, and destroying others for my greed. My executioner is allowing me to ----- die painlessly-- to enter Hell quietly." Dixon's quivering lips managed to whisper out his lines as he watched Ricky in forlorn hope that he might be spared, only to see him once again go into his briefcase. Dixon's eyes once again widened with fear as Ricky brought out a plastic beaker with a lid.

"No! Please don't! I'm begging you." His eyes scoured the room frantically, searching, desperate for a means, any means of escape. There was none and he swayed his head wildly from side to side as Ricky walked towards him with the poison. Ricky put down the poison and picked up the tape, cut a piece from it and walked towards Dixon. "Okay, so you want to die in agony: that's your choice."

"No please, I'll drink it!, I'll drink it!" He knew his fate: No hope of reprieve and with an air of fearful resignation reluctantly allowed the poison to be administered as his slipping away was recorded with only the gloves and sleeves of the killer on view. The pimp's head fell forward. The body slumped, only held aloft by the nails securing his hands to the door frame. A tear fell away from Ricky's eyes. "If only I could have persuaded Jack to find the strength from somewhere to forgive Dixon and therefore save his soul instead of sending him to Hell."

CHAPTER FIFTEEN

Jack sat at the table, a saddened look spread across his face. He could sense the depression creeping upon him again and knew he needed to start taking his medication but was aware that if he did, it would affect him mentally making him more relaxed, and he needed the edge the medication deprived him of to allow him to avenge Karina. He held her photograph before him for several minutes and set it back down, picking up her negligee burying his face into it; the knowledge of it being Karina's was enough to feel he was back in her presence. The tears flowed again as they did most days. His mental health was deteriorating but he somehow managed to keep it hidden. He had to keep going.

Outwardly he appeared well, though no-one could know the screaming that reverberated deep inside.

Arnold assembled the team into the main

incident room. "He's killed number three. I received this video via mobile phone twenty minutes ago. It shows the victim being poisoned whilst bound."

D.C.I. Arnold played out Dixon's last moments.

Revolted by what they saw, the air thick, disbelief on their faces the team sat in silence. D.S. Derek Smith commented "With all the circumstantial evidence surrounding Jack Green and knowing that we suspect he's the killer, surely he wouldn't sneak out to kill again, especially from under the noses of the surveillance team, but there can't be a third person involved."

"We have to catch this sick bastard. What kind of threat could he have possibly made to persuade the victim to voluntarily end his own life seeing the fear in his eyes." one distraught detective uttered, not wanting to watch the screen, but unable to look away.

The news on the murder was broadcast and within five minutes, Petra, one of the prostitutes that Dixon controlled rang the police after seeing it. The body was discovered soon after and the street immediately sealed off. The murder had taken place in Birmingham, approximately

IN THE NAME OF KARINA

twenty three miles from where Holland had been killed in Coventry where the police had been staking out the red light district.

Shaun Dixon's computer and mobile phone were taken apart without any connection linking him to Joe Holland, the drug dealer. The team interviewed all his prostitutes but no one knew of Holland.

Forensics once again found nothing inside or outside of Dixon's house. The only fingerprints, footprints, and clothing fibres belonged to Dixon, and hairs, that after analysis only came from him as did the blood.

His neighbours were interviewed and two of them remembered seeing a small red car with dark rear windows parked outside of their houses for several hours on different days. One neighbour wasn't sure of the make of car but the other one remembered that it was a Fiat Punto.

D.S. Kate Jones stated "Jack Green can't have done it, even if he'd managed to sneak past our guys, his car didn't move and the neighbour stated it was definitely red and not orange."

The neighbour also got a good look at the

123

driver when he stepped out to open the boot. He was interviewed in the temporary murder unit set up outside of Dixon's home.

"How would you describe him?" D.S. Jones. Had asked.

"I'd say he was in his late twenties with dark hair that receded in a strange shape."

"You must have been pretty close to observe that."

"Yes I was. I had come in from the back garden down the side of the house to pick some litter up that had blown in, when the driver climbed out of his car, so I was reasonably close to him without him being able to see me. He had dark glasses on and a pencil moustache."

"Would you recognise him again?"

"I might be able to."

"What was he wearing?"

"Dark blue jeans and a cream coloured sweater."

"Did he have trainers or shoes on?"

"I'm not sure, I couldn't see his feet."

"Did you notice any tattoos or other

distinguishing marks?"

"None at all but as I already told you with him wearing a sweater, only his hands and face were visible."

The D.S. thanked him for his help and left him with a police artist to help build up a computer generated likeness.

The areas around where the car had been parked were scrutinised but once again no clues emerged.

A press conference was hastily arranged, the photofit was released and hours later was on all news channels, with a fresh appeal for anyone to contact the police if they knew of anyone resembling the picture, especially if they had access to a red Fiat Punto with rear tinted windows.

Jack watched the broadcast in silence. Angry at being so sloppy, allowing someone to see him. The photo-fit suggested that he had a much fatter face and combined with the false moustache and dark glasses made it doubtful that anyone would recognise him from it but his planning had to be tighter as there was still much to be done to avenge Karina.

Over three hundred people rang in with a combined thirty different names, twenty four living in the Midlands area and they were given priority. Twenty more officers were assigned to the case and each address searched, as the named were brought in for questioning and to attend identity parades.

Shaun Dixon's neighbour discounted them all. Their mobile phone history was checked through the networks. Nothing was found to warrant anything further.

CHAPTER SIXTEEN

Jack sat alone in his bedroom thinking of his time with Karina. *I hope you are watching. I hope you can see. Three have gone already. Only three more to go. Your hateful stepfather is locked away without chance of clearing his name, but more importantly, both the drug dealer and pimp bastards are dead. I know you will be smiling, which warms my heart. In this mood I want to remember us, and so tomorrow, for two nights I have booked our favourite hotel at Skegness where we stayed twice. I'll retrace our footsteps; eat where we ate, drink at the cocktail bar that we found and walk along the promenade where we were hand in hand. Karina you are always in my thoughts and when vengeance is complete I will return to your side, to be with you forever.*

The following morning Jack opened up his suitcase, carefully folding up, and placing Karina's jumper, negligee and pillowcase inside, none of which he had washed since the day she

departed. He took the photograph of her that he most loved, and after kissing it placed it between his own clothes in the case. Jack put the case in the boot and after placing her watch on the dashboard, drove through to Skegness.

At the hotel reception he signed in for both himself and Karina.

"I'm sorry. I know you asked for a double bed, but being insistent on room thirty two, there are only two single beds in that room. Would you care to switch rooms?" asked the receptionist.

"No!!" was sharply delivered back, followed by Jack appearing to look upwards, embarrassed, as if offering apology to Karina. He looked back down and in a softer tone said, " it has to be number thirty two."

Jack entered the third floor room, stopping in the doorway, looking in, taking in the décor and the view, pleased that nothing had changed apart from the beds. He once again looked upwards and smiled, before he blew a kiss to Karina.

He unpacked the case, carefully slipping

her pillow case over the one on her bed. He straightened her negligee out, laying it along the length of her bed and finished by placing her jumper on the settee, next to where he would sit.

Although the day was cold, the sun was bright and low on the late Autumn afternoon as Jack walked along the promenade, Karina's gloves clasped tightly in his hand, and a smile on his face. He walked back and forth for over an hour, talking to himself about their time together, drawing strange glances from people passing by.

He stopped at a restaurant they used to eat at, sat down and asked for a menu. A short while later he beckoned the waiter across, ordering a well done rump steak, and a vegetarian lasagna with salad and garlic bread, Karina's favourite. He also ordered a bottle of house red. The waiter asked if they should wait with the food while his friend turned up.

"No. We'll have it as soon as it's ready. Thank you."

The waiter returned with the wine and Jack poured out two glasses.

After finishing his steak, he gave a deep sigh.

Karina it's not the same. It's not as I imagined it would be.

He took money from his wallet, placed it upon the table and left. On his way back to the hotel, the smile on his face was missing until he spotted the cocktail bar they both liked. Once inside he looked through the drinks menu and ordered two Bloody Mary's.

As jack sipped at his drink, he looked at Karina's full glass and a tear left his eye. Without finishing his drink he returned to the hotel. He stared deeply at her photograph, took a hold of her negligee, climbed into bed, resting his head on her pillow case and went to sleep.

In the morning he awoke and stared at the ceiling. "It's gone. The feeling's gone. It's just not the same. Those bastards will pay."

He quickly dressed, packed his case, paid the bill, and drove home, his head in angry place.

CHAPTER SEVENTEEN

Jack, assuming the name John Bell, called Martin Farrell to confirm their meeting was still on at his studio for three pm. He had stalked Farrell for four days and knew that he would be alone in his office at that precise time. The photographic studio was situated in a small disused church on the outer edges of Wolverhampton, converted into two levels; his living space at the back end of the bottom floor; his studio and offices above. Farrel had told John to go straight up as the main door would be unlocked.

Jack pulled into the secluded church yard and stopped the car. They hadn't passed anyone for over a mile. He looked all around checking that there were no c.c.t.v. cameras and drove further on after assuring himself that it was safe. He parked the car at the side of the church away from the windows so that Ricky could change his clothes without being noticed.

Jack was sweating, certain in what had to be done, though scared that he would be offending God by taking revenge here. He had tried to come up with an alternative place of execution, but couldn't find anywhere they could be alone. Convinced that it would be acceptable, someone had to stop what took place in the former house of prayer. He believed God would give his blessing.

"Stop panicking. I'm the one punishing him." said Ricky.

"But it still doesn't feel right."

He pushed open the heavy oak door, eerily creaking with every inch of it's opening.

Ricky stood quietly in the church and looked all around. The sun's rays danced through the tall stained glass windows painting shadowy patterns on the grey stone floor. After locking the door behind he quickly climbed the spiral staircase onto the landing of a first floor that Farrell had built.

"Come through John." Farrell shouted, not seeing him but guiding him towards the office by voice alone.

Ricky entered the doorway and stopped, his hands behind his back.

"What the hell's that on your head?" Farrell asked with an inquisitive voice, half smiling. The silence immediately removed his grin and he looked again at the balaclava. "What's this about? Who are you really?"

The silence remained. The deep stare intensified.

"I don't know what this is but I am expecting clients to arrive at any moment."

"John Bell?

Farrell's fear heightened. "I have no money on the premises and I want you to leave immediately or I'll call the police."

In his dark green overall, Ricky remained still, only watching. A dread rose up inside Farrell. He now knew that the intruder who had taken the time to make an appointment was more than just a thief. "I'm going to call the police." He made certain the desk was between himself and the intruder. "What's behind your back? Please I'm asking you; just go."

Ricky screamed "Who the hell do you think you are? You violate the house of God, torture your unsuspecting victims, capturing that on film and peddle your filth!"

Farrell grabbed a heavy paperweight with one hand, lifting the phone off the receiver with the other, accidentally knocking his cup of coffee over in his haste, his eyes wide, his body taut with fear.

"Have you any idea of how low the women sank after you finished your perverted acts of depravity? Did you care if they could ever smile again? Were you aware if any took their own lives not being able to live with themselves? You don't care, you have no conscience, but today you have consequence."

"Look I've got money. Can't we come to some sort of arrangement? "

"Money!! This isn't about money! The name Karina; mean anything to you?"

Farrell thought deeply, eager to be able to remember. His concentrated look angered Ricky who threw a photo of Karina towards him. "Do you recognise her now?" It was obvious that he did not.

"How many poor women have you degraded?"

A cold sweat engulfed Farrell. Ricky said no more, only glaring once again with a deeper hatred.

Farrell broke the silence. "All that was a long time ago. A time I deeply regret. I only take photographs now on a professional business basis."

"I know. I've seen the prints. You have a growing reputation for beautifully capturing waterways and waterfalls. The natural beauty in your pictures belies the person you really are."

Farrell tightened his grip on the paperweight as Ricky brought a tazer gun out from behind his back.

"Did you ever listen to them? begging you not to hurt them. Today is your day of reckoning. You are to spend eternity in the jaws of hell."

Farrell threw the paperweight at Ricky's head as he tried running for the door. It glanced off his lip making him wince but he instantly recovered. Before Farrell could escape he sent him crashing to the floor with a high voltage burst to his back. As Farrell lay dazed, Ricky put a cloth, soaked in chloroform, over his nose and held it in place until his body ceased moving.

When he came to, his senses slowly returned to normal. He tried standing up from the chair he was sat in. He couldn't move; his hands were tethered tightly to the arms of the heavy winged chair as his feet were to the chair legs. His head was restricted from moving in any direction, with padding between his head and the chairs wings, held fast by strong tape wound around the top of the chair binding his head and the chair as one. Farrell could only move his eyes which scanned from side to side; up and down without seeing anyone, his ears pricked without hearing the slightest sound. His breathing heightened. His panic grew.

Several minutes later Ricky spoke from the back of the room, making Farrell's eyes switch from side to side, desperate to see him but totally unable to turn his head. "Some years ago a twenty two year old woman answered an advertisement for a photographic model. The work was for a leading national fashion catalogue, ---- supposedly. She moved here from

Birmingham, desperate to rebuild her life. The only time she tried to climb out of the gutter. The only time she made a real effort to be rid of the drugs that dictated her young life. At that point in time she needed someone genuine on her side. Instead she put her trust in you-----"

"I don't know wh------"

"Shut the fuck up!!" Ricky screamed, and in anger rushed at Farrell grabbing his hair attempting to pull it backward viciously, the tape not allowing his head to move. The pain closed Farrell's eyes tightly as his teeth clenched rigidly together as a strong peg was forced onto his nose which opened his eyes wide in fear. Ricky shouted out like a maniac, "If you talk again without being told to, I'll cut your fucking tongue out!"

Farrell sat completely still in frightened shock apart from his heart that felt like it was trying to burst free from his chest.

"As I said, she put her trust in you. You could have saved her. Instead, when she left she was beyond help from anyone. You more than any other person are responsible for Karina's downfall, and you did it all in a house of

God. Later, totally downtrodden she moved into my friend's spare room, penniless and without hope. She explained how you drugged her before forcing her into sadomasochistic poses. For her pain you gave her good money, knowing well she would be back for more, especially fuelled by the need for drugs. It was a cycle that you relied upon, one from which she could not break.

She slowly sank lower and lower until you cast her aside, no longer able to purchase the drugs she had become totally reliant upon."

Ricky forced strong sticky tape across Farrell's mouth rendering him unable to breathe. "You like pain and fear intermingling so I'm going to spoil you. I'm going to give you as much as you can endure, Plus it's your lucky day; I'm going to stretch it out for hours, and seeing as how you like pictures of water so much, I've decided to treat you to a pitcher of water."

He attempted to rock his head to release it from its vice like bonds without success. The tape around it remained secure and the panic within him was plainly visible, his pupils fully dilated as Farrell tried twisting and turning his body, arms and legs, desperate for air. The more panic, the greater the desperation.

Ricky walked around to face Farrell. After watching him squirming, his lungs ready to burst, Ricky inserted a tiny hole in the tape allowing him to breathe. Farrell sucked the air in deeply but as he did so a blindfold was pulled over his eyes, fear pushing up his breathing rate even further. Ricky remained still and quiet for twenty minutes allowing Farrell's mind to imagine every dreaded act, increasing the fear until eventually his chest, which appeared to be pounding out of control, slowed down.

At this point a small plastic tube was inserted into the tape over his mouth creating further panic in Farrell.

Ricky stood quietly by once again until his breathing calmed down at which point he immersed the other end of the tube into a small bowl of water that Farrell unknowingly sucked up, expecting air, immediately spluttering it back through the tube coughing and choking as Ricky took the water away. He nearly removed the tape, convinced Farrell was going to pass out but delayed doing so for a few seconds until his breathing through the tube became normal again. He would not be allowed such a quick death; there was too much hatred in Jack.

After several minutes Ricky re-introduced the water again. The spluttering and choking continued intermittently for two hours, when Ricky had to remove the tape for a third time, allowing Farrell to vomit violently. New tape was put over his mouth. His blindfold was removed and the video footage of his suffering was replayed back to him from Ricky's mobile.

"You're experiencing similar fear to that you subjected your victims to but your pain in this life is nearly over. This punishment will be child's play for what you receive in Hell. I'll make you take your final breaths until your lungs burst: You're a photographer, can you picture that? Actually you won't need to, I'm leaving the blindfold off so you can see as the water rises through the clear tube that will explode your lungs."

Farrell tried in vain with all his might to break free from his bonds as he watched Ricky place the tube back into the bowl. He initially refused to draw breath but unable to either spit the tube away or topple the water, with a last despairing pleading look, begged Ricky for mercy. It was met with a cold unshifting stare. The water rose up the tube, his death recorded on the mobile.

Ricky searched quickly through his office and living area, as Jack had asked him to do, to try to find any photographs that Karina may have been on. Jack couldn't afford for them to fall into police hands.

After half an hour Ricky came away empty handed.

Arriving home later Ricky went for a shower. Panic hit him: He saw in the mirror a slight cut on his lip where the paperweight had caught him leaving a spot of dried blood. His mind raced feverishly; *would there be any at Farrell's?; should I go back and check?; would I even find it?* He looked again at his lip and decided that it was such a tiny scratch, there would have been no blood spilt.

Jack realised that although Ricky couldn't find any photographs, the police might and he couldn't take the chance of their discovering her photographs at his own place before his work was finished so he needed to destroy all of her photo's.

"I hope you rot in Hell. You've taken Karina

away from me twice now."

CHAPTER EIGHTEEN

When the video was transferred to Arnold's phone, the team once again watched in horror. Most were too shocked to speak. Two officers, one a woman had their eyes fill up with tears, another rushed to the toilet and was physically sick.

After releasing Farrell's picture it wasn't long before they had his identity and the church was taped off.

When the pathologist and forensics had finished at the crime scene, the police searched the premises and discovered a large quantity of obscene photographs taken in the crypt that had been turned into a dungeon. A ledger was discovered that bore the names and addresses under separate headings of customers and photographic models. This was an important find, and along with other items, was taken away. Also a tiny drop of fresh blood had been discovered by forensics on the wooden floor but there was no external injury to Farell.

The team were assembled back at Headquarters where the white board displayed the murdered victims photo's, times, dates, places and methods of their demise. Also listed were all the names and addresses of everyone who had been interviewed and had their houses searched.

"Right Sarah I want you to concentrate on the ledger. I want facial images from the pictures that we found, cross referenced to the models addresses. I want you to determine if any of the women have lived in two or possibly three of the areas where the murders took place. I need you to find out if any of the women in the photo's are now dead; If any are, I want all previous addresses.

"Harry I want you to lead a team of six to interview Farrell's family, neighbours and friends. Find out if he's ever been threatened by anyone. Whoever did this, knowing what his wife went through, would have been round for him before now. Jane, take one of the team and concentrate on Farrell's customers from the ledger to find out if they know anything. Talk with them privately at first because they'll be giving nothing away; then lean on them to come up with something unless they want their next interview to be at their home. That'll get them twitching. Derek and Kate, the murderer or his wife is connected to all three crime areas. I want you to cross reference the voting register and council tax register for these areas for anyone at all that lived in any two of them and hopefully you'll come across someone that lived in all three."

Jane Morgan said "The methods that he's using are getting progressively worse each time but Farrell's place of murder baffles me. From the religious overtones in the previous notes, I would have thought his mental state would not have allowed him to kill in a church, especially in that torturous manner. I think what D.S. Smith half suggested, before we released Jack Green, the possibility of being three involved could actually be a reality. It may not be out of the question that Stamp has a second accomplice."

Apart from the blood, a light footprint was found close to the body imprinted into the dried spilt coffee from a trainer of the same size left down the alley, where Holland's murderer's car was parked, although a different tread to the one found at the previous crime scene but It didn't match Farrell's footwear and was a size smaller. Also two tiny strands of a dark green cotton fibre were attached to one of the discarded tapes that had been over Farrell's mouth.

Jack Green was brought in for further questioning but after his house was searched again, with nothing found, he was released.

Two days later Sarah finished going through the ledger's photographic models "Of the eighteen women in the photo's, six couldn't be Identified, although four were recognised by the other women we interviewed leaving two that we don't know about. We have no idea what period of time his activities covered. Of those we traced only two of the women lived in two of the three areas involved in the killings. Both are married but weren't when the photo's were taken and nobody lived in all three areas."

The results from the cotton fibres were returned, being so widespread their origin couldn't be confirmed.

The two remaining unidentified models photographs were released to the media resulting in them both being located, safe and well and both married.

After analysis, the spot of blood proved to be different to the victim's blood group, but also different to Jack Green's DNA, and had no match on the data base. The blood was the second major slip up by the killers.

The officers checking the voting and council tax registers came up with forty two people of the general public who had lived in two areas and nine people who had lived in all three areas, with six of them not on the voting register. Arnold informed the police teams to either get permission from the householders to have their homes searched or be put under arrest on suspicion of murder where an immediate section eighteen would come into force, an inspectors authority, that had no need for a search warrant to be issued.

"Anyone unwilling to comply will definitely have something to hide. Also, a voluntary DNA sample is required from them and again if anyone refuses, warn them they will be arrested, again on suspicion of murder where they then can't refuse to give a DNA sample."

Everyone was taken in for questioning across five police stations. Shaun Dixon's neighbour visited each of the stations to attend identity parades but never hesitated over any one of them. It was becoming a mammoth murder enquiry as each one in turn was interviewed. Two people were registered as owning a red Fiat Punto, both of the six not on the voting register, one being Ivan Jovanovic who had been interviewed earlier, living close to where Holland lived, but was not required for a second interview as it was proven that he was out of the country at the time of the first two murders. The second person named Tony Jack.

At police headquarters the DCI had five of the six present who had lived in all three areas. Still working in their respective teams Sarah and a colleague interviewed a Mr. Howard Smith. It emerged that he had been married for ten years; he couldn't drive; he had solid alibi's for three of the four murders and his hair was naturally ginger. He was eliminated.

Kate and Derek questioned Simon Barnes. "Mr. Barnes are you married?"

"No I'm divorced."

"When did you get divorced?"

"Nearly four years ago."

"Do you know where your ex wife is at present?"

"What the Hell's this all about? Has something happened to her?"

"Not at all. These are just routine questions."

"I haven't got a clue where she is and I don't want to know."

"Have you ever owned a red Fiat car?"

"No, I drive a Corsa 1000 cc. I've had it for three years."

"What colour is it?"

"It's red."

"You moved address from Coventry to Birmingham in nineteen ninety five. What was the reason for the move?"

Barnes hesitated before responding. "I moved to be near friends." he said warily.

"Around nineteen ninety nine you moved again to Wolverhampton. For what reason?"

A troubled look came to his face. "I don't get it. What's all this about? Do I need a solicitor present?"

"Mr. Barnes, you're only helping us with our enquiries. Do you feel that you need a solicitor with you? You can certainly have one if you do."

Barnes saw the look that Derek gave him, a sort of --you get a solicitor and you're guilty look. He continued. "I moved to be nearer to my father who was ill."

"Where were you on the night on the fifth of November?"

"I'm starting to feel uneasy, I think I'll ring my brief if that's okay?"

"That's not a problem but the only reason that you're helping us is because of the areas you've lived in. Another forty people are helping us by answering the same questions as they also lived in the same areas."

"I can't remember where I was that night."

"Where were you on the night of the fifteenth of November?"

"That's easy. I was in Glasgow on company

business. I know because it was the company centenary and I spent it alone."

"What were you doing on the evening of the twenty seventh of November?"

"I remember that night. It was my best friends fiftieth birthday. We went to his favourite Chinese restaurant before we all went back to his place until about four in the morning; he'll clarify that."

"And on the sixth of December?"

Barnes took out his mobile phone and got his personal organiser up. "Thought so! I was in London on business for three days."

"We'd like to examine your mobile phone later. Can anyone confirm these places and times?"

"Yes my boss, he'll verify it. I'll also give you the name of the hotel where I stayed."

"Could I ask the reason for your not registering to vote?"

"It doesn't interest me one little bit. They are all the same, promise the earth; deliver nothing."

"Mr. Barnes, finally we'd like to take a mouth swab for your DNA."

"That's no problem" he replied.

As Barnes sample was being taken, in another room his alibi's were being cross checked with his employer and the hotel. Barnes was thanked and later allowed to leave after his home had been searched.

"He seemed on edge all the time."

"I agree Derek and he had a dark receding hairline and a small red car albeit the wrong make, although similar but his alibi's definitely check out. He's in the clear."

D.I. Harry Turner interviewed Tony Jack accompanied by D.C. Jane Morgan as Arnold looked in on it from the outside. Upon inspection his red Fiat Punto was found to have rear tinted windows and was taken in for forensic scrutiny. It appeared to have had a recent valet, with the tyres re-blacked.

Harry Turner began the questioning. "Mr. Jack, you are helping with our inquiries, regarding the areas you have lived in. You lived in Birmingham before moving to Wolverhampton. What was the purpose for that move?"

"I decided that I needed a complete change of

location as I was being harassed by neighbours at that address as I had been in my previous home in Birmingham."

"What was all the harassment for?"

Jack shrugged his shoulders. "Some people get picked on all the time. I don't know; maybe they felt I didn't fit in."

"Why in two thousand and four did you go to live in Coventry?" asked the D.I.

"I got married and my wife liked the place so we just uprooted having no strong ties in Wolverhampton."

"Where were you on the fifth of November?"

"I really can't remember."

"And your whereabouts on the fifteenth of November?"

Jack gave both officers a slow curious look before answering. "Once again I'm not really sure. What's with all the questions? This isn't only around where I lived. Am I under suspicion for something?"

"At this stage, no, but we are checking your car as the same type of car with dark rear windows has been involved with several crimes, so it is really important that you think about your whereabouts on these dates plus what you were doing on the twenty seventh of November and the sixth of December."

"That was only a few days ago; I was at home alone."

"Would your wife have any recollection of your movements?"

"My wife was killed several years ago by a hit and run driver."

"I'm sorry to hear that Mr. Jack, but it is essential that you try to recall your movements. It has been noted that your car appears to have been thoroughly valeted, including your tyres re-blacked.why is that?"

"Yes, I've had it professionally cleaned as I'm about to try to sell it."

"I see from your records that you've been to court twice for kerb crawling." D.I. Turner stopped talking, watching Tony Jack, eager to see his response. There was none. "Are these not your records? Weren't you up at court?"

"It's not something I'm proud of. I don't make

friends easily and I don't want to get close to anyone. No one could take the place of my wife, but I still have needs."

"We require you to give us a voluntary DNA sample."

He eyed D.S. Morgan up, and then slowly nodded.

"Tony Jack I am concluding this interview but am holding you in custody until forensics have finished their examination of your car and your house has been fully searched."

Although Jack couldn't remember his whereabouts on the dates in question he was released twenty four hours later.

D.S. Scott Andrews led with the interview of Mike Robinson, another who had lived in all three areas.

"Mr. Robinson are you married?"

"No. I was meant to get married as I lived with my girlfriend but she was unfortunately killed in an accident years ago."

"Do you own a red Fiat car?"

"No I drive a silver Ford Mondeo. I've had it for about five years. I can't believe I'm in for questioning and my house being searched. What's it all about? You've definitely got me mixed up with someone else."

"Mr. Robinson you're one of many who are being questioned in relation to where you've lived over the years. You moved from Coventry to Birmingham When and why did you move?"

"I moved to be closer to work in ninety seven."

"You also changed address from Birmingham to Wolverhampton. What was the reason on that occasion?"

"I was made redundant and couldn't afford to live there any longer and moved to share a place with a friend which was more manageable before I eventually moved back to Coventry."

"Can you tell me why you're not on the voting register?"

"I just never got around to it. These things are always cut and dried anyway plus I support a minority party so one vote wouldn't make any difference."

Scott asked "On the evening of the fifth of November, where were you?"

"I haven't got a clue."

"On the night of the fifteenth of November what were you doing?"

"We're talking nearly four weeks ago; I honestly don't know."

"On the twenty seventh of November where were you?" asked Scott.

" I remember that night, I watched a film. It's my chill night".

"Who would have been with you to verify it?"

"No-one."

"On the sixth of December in the daytime, can you remember your whereabouts?"

"That was only a week ago. I stayed in again by myself.

"That's two nights you can't remember, one day and night you were at home alone. Can anyone confirm   your whereabouts at those times?"

"Certainly not the times I was at home. I can't think of anyone that could verify where I was on the fifth and fifteenth of November, if there is someone it will come to me."

"Could we examine your mobile telephone?"

"I don't possess one and never have."

"Could we have a sample of your DNA Mr. Robinson?" Scott asked.

"Why would you need that? No, I don't think so."

"Mr. Robinson you can't refuse us. Why would you want to?"

"I have done nothing wrong and it will remain on the data base."

Scott reassured him. "Once our enquiries come to a satisfactory conclusion all the DNA samples taken will be destroyed if given voluntarily, but if not, we would arrest you to legally take one which would then remain on the data base. It only requires us to take a mouth swab."

Robinson apologised and the mouth swab was taken before he was allowed to leave and his name like all the others was added to a list of three possibilities. -1-In the clear. -2- Doubtful. -3-possible.

He was entered under the doubtful column. "If he comes up with anyone that can verify his alibi's then we can safely move his name across to the -in the clear section-. Wrong car; totally bald and never married. I think he should already be in that category. I don't know how the rest of the other interviews are going but I have a feeling we won't end up with a suspect from this line of enquiry" Scott frustratingly said to his colleagues.

A fifth person to help the police, Brian Chandler, was marked down in the clear section as he was confined to a wheelchair and after consulting with his doctor found he had been incapacitated for over two years.

Detective Inspector Harry Turner, surrounded by several colleagues took a sip of his coffee whilst stood next to the vending machine. "Arnold's an arsehole. Every time he thinks he's got the right man. Do you remember the Abbey National Building Society robbery? Nothing to go on but a gut instinct: Ronny Evans; Arnold was ready to hang draw and quarter him. He forced his opinion on everyone. What a bloody idiot he looked when it came to light that Evans just happened to be in police custody overnight in Liverpool at the time. Even then Arnold trying to save face said that he was definitely involved in the planning of the robbery. The man's a buffoon. How does he keep getting these cases?"

Three days later the desk sergeant walked into Arnolds office. "Sir a call came through an hour ago about a red Fiat Punto with tinted rear windows that is always parked on an allotment, most of the time under a protective sheet. A patrol car was sent to investigate and checked the registration. The owner is a woman; Sharon Smith, but the address it's registered to is the same address as Mike Robinson, already questioned having lived in all three areas where the murders were committed."

Arnold paused for thought. "Bring them both in. Scott interviewed him; I'll get an update from him and listen to the taped interview."

When Robinson was brought in Arnold was informed that the female owner had been dead for around four years.

D.S. Scott Andrews re-interviewed Robinson. "Why didn't you inform us of your hideaway when we searched your home?"

"Firstly it's not a hideaway; secondly I thought the search was solely for the house and thirdly I'd nothing to hide in the first place."

"Why did you lie about owning a red Fiat Punto?"

"I didn't lie. The car belonged to my girlfriend. It was her pride and joy and I would never get rid of it. It's still my girlfriend's car and I wouldn't dream of changing it to my name; I feel her presence in the car but you wouldn't understand that."

"You explained in your interview that she is deceased. What was her name?"

"Sharon Smith."

"What about road tax and insurance?"

"Like I say it was her car and still is. It's all I've got left of her. I do everything around it in her name. Okay it might be wrong but I'm really doing no harm by it except keeping her memory alive."

"Do you clean the car on a regular basis?"

"My girlfriend was extremely proud of her car and I thoroughly clean it both inside and outside as she did".

"Has the vehicle always had the rear windows tinted?"

"They were like that when she bought the car."

"We will search your allotment area with its sheds. Is there anything that you would like to tell us before we conduct the search and forensics examine the car?"

"I have already told you, I've got nothing to hide."

Scott eyed Robinson in silence. He glared back, neither man breaking the stare.

Robinson was read out his rights before being led away.

Scott's colleague spoke up. "Even with thorough cleaning of the Punto I wonder if we'll come up with a second set of prints or any clue that might shed light on the theory that there could possibly be three people involved in the murders?"

" Three!! Bloody four; that is if the unsolved blood sample left at Farrell's actually belongs to anyone that was a threat to Farrell in the first place because it doesn't match up with

Robinson's, Jack Green's or Tony Jack's DNA. This investigation is going backwards."

The D.V.L.A. were contacted regarding Robinson's girlfriend's driving licence and the Fiat Punto registration document, but the driving licence was only a paper one, with no photograph, and the address, after checking it out turned out to be a flat she rented many years earlier, her original neighbours not recognising Mike Robinson's picture.

Only the suspect's fingerprints were found in the car with no other DNA emerging other than Robinson's from hair and skin dust. Robinson was sat stony faced next to his solicitor as D.S. Scott Andrews started another bout of questioning. "In your allotment shed we've discovered three brand new pairs of overalls unopened. Why would you have that many?"

"Is this a wind up? I can't even remember when I bought them; possibly got three for the price of two" he said with a sarcastic grin.

The D.S. looked through him, and although angry inside he never took the bait. "We also found two brand new balaclavas still in their wrappers. You haven't got two heads have you."

Robinson, upset with all the police activity that had recently taken place in his life only returned the icy stare back in silence.

"Why would you purchase two of an item that would never wear out?"

"Once again maybe the price was right, I can't remember."

"What do you use balaclavas for?"

"I do a lot of work down at the allotment in a winter and it gets really cold out in the open."

"Where is the one that is in present use? It's not in the shed."

"That's why I purchased another. I spilt oil on the old one and so destroyed it."

"On your furnace Mr. Robinson?"

"Yes that's right."

"Do you use your furnace to get rid of much rubbish?"

"I use it occasionally."

"Although it's not new can you explain why it's in a virtual pristine like condition without any trace of ash or burnt remains?"

The solicitor broke in "D.S. Andrews can you explain where this line of questioning is going. My client is------"

"I can assure you that these questions are very relevant" interrupted the D.S. irately as his tone rose,"and I will pursue them. I repeat, where did you put the ashes from the incinerator?"

"Occasionally I clean it out bagging them up and throwing them out with my household refuse."

"At the allotment shed we came across two boxed pairs of trainers. Two for the price of one I suppose?We also discovered two brand new mobile phones, yet when first questioned you said you didn't own one."

"I don't. I bought the trainers and mobiles for my twin nephews. It's their birthday in two weeks time and my sister agreed to me buying them as she struggles financially. Check it out with her; she'll also confirm their shoe size."

"Why would they be in your shed and not your home?"

"I may have taken them out of the car and got

on with some work. I can't remember."

"Mr. Robinson a red Fiat Punto with rear tinted windows has been used in at least two murders that have taken place in and around the Midlands area."

"That's coincidence, it has absolutely nothing to do with my girlfriend's car. Punto's are an extremely popular vehicle. They're all over the place; there must be hundreds of them with darkened windows."

"So you drive the late Ms. Smiths car, even though you are not insured. Why not drive your Mondeo?"

"I insure it in her name, and my Mondeo cover allows me drive any other car."

"That's okay then if a dead woman's given you her permission; I don't know what the insurance company's take on that would be."

" I only take it out now and then just to keep it ticking over."

"And so the M.O.T. certificate will show it's not been driven for many miles?"

"I'll dig the paperwork out for you."

"When you were first interviewed you couldn't come up with anyone who could verify your whereabouts at the time of the murders. Having had time to think, did anyone come to mind?"

"No, not at all."

"We found no photographs of you at your home. Is that because you changed your hairstyle and shaved the moustache off?"

"I occasionally grow my hair in a short crop though mostly have it shaven but I have never had a moustache."

"Which hairdresser do you use?"

"I don't. I shave it myself."

"Very fortunate."

"Not fortunate at all; just practical."

"We found a pair of sunglasses in your fiancés car, similar to the ones described by a witness as being worn by the driver of a red Punto parked near to the scene of Shaun Dixon's murder. I would think dark glasses would be a must for you, having different coloured eyes. Without the shades no-one would fail to recognise you even without the moustache and dark receding hairline that existed there before."

"Out of the millions and millions of sunglasses around there must only be four or five styles. I'm getting fed up of your ridiculous questions and stupid innuendoes. I've done nothing wrong and you damn well know it. You'd love to nail me for the murders that you can't resolve. What's the problem; lot of heat coming from upstairs is there? There's not a single shred of evidence to suggest my Involvement."

Robinson turned to his solicitor. "How long can this idiot keep me here for?"

D.S. Andrews smiled at Robinson.

His solicitor spoke up. " As far as I can ascertain, you have no evidence to suggest my clients involvement and you are running out of time in which to hold him. I suggest to you that you allow him to leave and concentrate on trying to find the real killer."

" I will conclude the interview with him but will continue to hold Robinson while our investigation continues, and if need be, will ask the court for more time to hold him." Added the D.S.

"My client has already submitted a DNA sample which must obviously have proved negative. How long is this hounding to go on for?"

"Your client's DNA did not match that found at one of the murder scenes but there is a strong possibility that an accomplice was present at the murders."

"You've already charged one man with murder. John Stamp. My clients DNA doesn't fit; are you suggesting that there's a gang of God knows how many murderers going round the Midlands killing people?"

"Until I am told that no evidence has come to light at both Mr. Robinson's home and his allotment, I will continue to hold him as long as the court allows."

When no evidence could be found to link Mike Robinson to the crime, Arnold thumped his desk and gave the order for his release. "I want twenty four hour surveillance on Jack Green, Tony Jack and Mike Robinson."

"He's losing it again" remarked D.I. Harry Turner.

CHAPTER NINETEEN

Jack's handkerchief was sodden, but the flow could not be stemmed; his face around the eyes a deep red, the depression was getting worse, the time between depressive bouts, shorter. He held on tightly to Karina's silver watch, imagining he was holding her hand. How he wished they were still together. He remembered her stories from when she was young. *Not many happy times for her growing up;* He remembered the stories of the beatings her stepfather gave her and the times she was left on her own, sometimes for days. *The love she craved; the love she had to give.* He compared it to his own childhood; no difference.

Jack got drunk that night and In his anger decided that in the morning he would start planning the elimination of number five, the strip club owner, while Ricky was away for nearly a fortnight..

Opening his bedroom curtains in the

morning he glanced out of the window and noticed the car parked opposite, was still there. It had been there from the previous night with two people sat inside. A frown appeared on his brow, the suspicion aroused in him. He made a point of going out through the front door to take something from his car so he would be seen. He then went back inside and left through the back door not bothering to open his lounge blinds. He emerged onto the alley and walked fifty metres before coming out onto the wasteland where he parked his van. He thought on the parked car and told himself he was being stupid; it was an ordinary car and only his over active imagination. Yet there were still two more to kill and he wouldn't take any chances of his plan failing. He drove off in the van towards Manchester and in case he was being watched, he set the timer to bring the lights on in the evening and off again in the morning at his home, so it appeared he was in, with Ricky being away.

The strip club was situated down a small street only fifty metres away from the bustling night life of the old town. Jack would watch Edmunds for two weeks, parking his van complete with false number plates, close to the club so that he could watch Edmunds' comings and goings. If a pattern emerged of his habits he would know where to strike. The strip club, although seedy was licensed but behind the main building an extension housed a massage parlour and brothel where Karina, years earlier had worked.

After keeping Edmunds under observation for two days he drove back to Coventry and parked back on the spare ground once again before entering his house from the back way. With his blinds still closed and wanting to keep them that way, he went upstairs and looked through his bedroom window to make certain that the suspect car was no longer there. "Damn! It's still there."

After panicking briefly he realised that no approach must have been made to the house or they would have realised that he had sneaked out the back way and they would have been watching that. He went out of the front door, taking something from his car before returning back inside.

Over the course of the next two weeks there was

aways a car overseeing the house, sometimes a different car, sometimes different people and usually parked in slightly different areas, but Jack knew they were on to him. Ricky returned to the house.

"Ricky you need to know that I might be being watched. If you don't want any further involvement, I appreciate everything you've done for me knowing that I couldn't do it. You must be the best friend a man could have."

"Jack I did it for you. I knew what I was getting into and I'll not slink away because the heat may be on. We'll have to be extra careful that's all. You continue to make the plans and I'll be there to execute them; literally."

It had become apparent to Jack that on a Friday and Saturday night, parties continued until the early hours, after which Edmunds would take a taxi back to the outskirts of Manchester where he lived in a large detached house. There were always people around, most likely partying there too though they could easily have been minders. He couldn't base his plans on the house. In the two weeks that Jack observed the strip club it appeared that Edmunds, on a Sunday, Monday and Tuesday would drive home in the early hours, usually with a different woman from the club. Wednesday and Thursday nights he drove home alone at around eleven p.m. before his club closed. With the one way driving system in place around the town Edmunds always took a short cut through a small derelict and desolate business park that bypassed the one way system saving approximately twenty minutes. He had to drive through narrow winding alleys that separated the empty buildings. At one point around a bend the alley was so narrow that he wouldn't even be able to open his car doors if he broke down.

After a lot of consideration Jack decided this would be the place to strike, although it required a lot more planning and preparation than any of his previous revenge attacks.

While in disguise Jack had purchased an old Volvo estate in York. It was a heavy vehicle that the plan required and its design was ideal. Jack had also been busily preparing the area ready to trap Edmunds, by knocking holes into the brickwork on the two adjacent buildings at the narrowest point on the disused business park.

He was ready, so Ricky could carry out his plan on Wednesday at eleven pm. approximately.

Ricky drove up in the Volvo, the van already parked out of view. He carefully pushed one end of a girder into the hole of the brickwork that Jack had prepared, until it was far enough through to allow the other end to be entered into the adjacent wall, and fed it back through until it was secured in position through both walls two feet from the ground, not allowing a car to be driven by.

Ricky waited in the Volvo, parked out of sight, until Edmunds drove up alone right on schedule.

He followed the car into the winding alleys.

The girder appeared in Edmunds' headlights at the last second but as he could only slowly turn around the bend it enabled him easily to stop but only an inch away from the steel beam. Before he had a chance to reverse, the Volvo stopped directly behind hitting the BMW, turning off the engine, putting it into gear and pulling on the handbrake, not allowing it to be shunted backwards as the Volvo was a sturdy vehicle and there was no ground for the BMW to build up any speed.

Ricky climbed out through the sunroof onto the bonnet as Edmunds looked back at him. Ricky smashed his rear window with a hammer as the club owner screamed at him. He quickly opened the drivers door to get out but it wedged tight against the wall with only a six inch gap. Edmunds threw open the passenger side door; the same. Ricky poured petrol into Edmund's car through the rear window as he frantically tried climbing over his seat into the rear of the car but not before a match was lit and then replaced into the matchbox, flaring up and being tossed into his car instantly engulfing the strip club owner in flames.

As Ricky walked back over the top of the Volvo, Edmunds shrill screams went unheeded. He then set the Volvo alight and briskly walked across to the waiting van and after going through the undressing procedure, Jack drove quietly away without speaking, knowing there was only one more to die in the name of Karina.

He destroyed all the clothing and footwear and the following morning drove out to two different tyre companies to have all the van's tyres replaced with part worn ones before parking the van on the wasteland and re-entering his house through the back door from the rear alleyway.

D.C.I. Arnold arrived home from work around ten pm. the following day.

"Have you eaten?" Fiona asked.

" No. I'm famished. When you get into something, you just drive yourself onwards not realising the time or even how hungry you've become."

Fiona brought a large well done rump steak dinner through for him on a tray, after pouring a beer out for him. His eyes followed her across to the chair she sat down in. "What's with the steak and waitress service?"

"Dave I've been thinking about something for a while now and I've made a decision. I rang Simon earlier this afternoon to ask if he still felt the same about donating one of his kidneys. I'm going to accept his offer, subject to all the tests being positive."

Dave put his tray down and held his wife. "I'm so glad you came to this decision. You'll have to ring the specialist to let him know so that he can get the ball rolling."

"I already have. I have to be at the hospital tomorrow just for a compatibility blood test as a formality. It's going to happen. I'm going to get my life back."

Dave squeezed her tightly.

CHAPTER TWENTY

Two days later a further letter was received at the station addressed to D.C.I. Arnold and the laboratory copied the wording and returned it to Coventry Central. Arnold read it out to the team.

EDMUNDS WAS NUMBER FIVE

ONLY ONE MORE STILL ALIVE

YOU WON'T CATCH ME UNTIL I'M DONE

BUT I'VE NOT BEAT YOU. I'VE NOT WON

ALL WE HAVE ARE LOSERS HERE

THE GUILTY, ME, AND MY WIFE SO DEAR
6--5

"Is that it?" D.S. Kate Jones asked."

"That's all there is" Arnold replied. "Who the hell is Edmunds? We've had no reported suspicious deaths in the area."

A minute later his file was on screen; "Manchester. The first one outside of the Midlands; why?"

D.C.I. Arnold accompanied by D.S. Derek Smith drove through to meet with his counterpart heading the Manchester murder inquiry and after they were briefed were taken to the crime scene.

"All the preparation with the brickwork" said Arnold scratching his head. "This killing's different; much more planning and forethought."

"We've checked all the local builders merchants to see if they've sold any second hand RSJ's. None of them handle any. We've tried all the scrap merchants, another dead end."

"And I bet you've not come across a single clue" said Arnold.

"Unfortunately you're right. Is that how it's been with his other victims?"

"Mostly. We've charged one with murder but there are others involved. A blood sample was found at one crime scene but at this stage we can't tie it in to anyone." Arnold had to admit.

He rang through to have Mike Robinson, Tony Jack and Jack Green brought in again for questioning and ordered their properties to be searched while they drove back to Coventry.

"They were the only suspects that we've been watching. Did they know they were under surveillance and sneaked out or should we be looking for someone else? I want to know if Robinson's burner has recently been used. If it has I want forensics to examine it and look around for any unburnt remains. Also check to see if he has the same number of balaclavas and overalls left in his shed. Check the mobiles and trainers have gone. I just hope forensics find brick dust in one of the properties to match that of the crime scene. I know the clothing will have been somehow destroyed but dust gets everywhere. If suspicious coincidences were enough we'd have all we need on all three men to virtually guarantee a conviction, but which one? It's not and if one of them was in the frame, we would still have no concrete evidence to go to court with; it's all circumstantial."

Jack Green was the first to be interviewed.

"Where were you on the fourth of January this year?"

"I was at home decorating."

"Can anyone substantiate that?" continued D.S. Sarah Brown

"You can have a look if you want."

"Don't get clever. You could be in a lot of trouble so if I were you I'd co-operate."

"I was by myself. I've been decorating for over a week now."

"Have you visited a DIY store during that time?"

"No I already had everything in that I needed. Why do you ask?"

"Have you set foot out of your house since you started decorating?"

"I can't recollect doing so. My fridge and freezer are always stocked up. Look I've done nothing wrong, where is this leading?"

"Do you know a strip club owner called Edmunds?"

"I've never heard of him."

"I see from the bandage that you've hurt your hand. What happened to it?"

"I built a York stone fireplace in the living

room and grazed my hand across it."

"I would like a doctor to examine it."

Green looked across to his solicitor who nodded his agreement to it. The interview was terminated and Green later allowed to leave after the injury proved inconclusive and his home searched again without result.

Mike Robinson was interviewed.

"Where were you on the fourth of January this year from midnight and all the following day?"

"I was at home. I haven't been out for nearly two weeks with flu like symptoms."

"Did you have a doctor visit you?"

"No. I just took all the usual remedies and gradually sweat it out."

"You appear okay now."

"I started feeling a lot better yesterday morning. I can't believe you're searching my house again. What are you hoping to find? My solicitor has advised me that I can remain silent especially as I have been totally co-operative in my first interview but I've nothing to hide so I will answer any questions that you ask."

"Do you know a John Edmunds from Manchester?"

"Not at all. I don't know anyone of that name. Who is he?"

"He's a strip club owner."

Robinson shook his head. From outside the interview room Dave Arnold studied Robinson's face and body language as he talked, desperately trying to spot any give away sign. It never faltered. D.I. Smith concluded the questioning and after both Robinson's home and allotment were searched, and hiding nothing, he was allowed to leave.

Tony Jack was interviewed, also stating that he had been at home for several days without venturing out and after a search of his house produced nothing, he was also released.

The following night the surveillance team noticed a red Fiat Punto with rear tinted windows parked several cars away from Robinsons house but it wasn't his girlfriends and after checking, discovered it belonged to Ivan Jovanovic, the details from the D.V.L.A. correctly being informed of a change of address.

They only lived ten doors apart. Arnold was informed but after consideration decided that it was a coincidence as the change of address was registered; there was no connection between him and Robinson, and Jovanovic was out of the country at the time of the previous murders.

CHAPTER TWENTY-ONE

Dave Arnold's wife rang through to the station needing to talk to him urgently. It concerned the blood sample given three days earlier for a compatibility test with her son's blood. The specialist had rung Fiona to ask her to come to the hospital to discuss the results. He advised her to bring someone with her and not to drive herself.

They were at the hospital within the hour where they were ushered through to his office.

"Mrs. Arnold, the results were returned from the laboratory a short while ago highlighting an extraordinary phenomenon. I have to tell you that your DNA is different to that of Simon's".

"What do you mean"? she asked.

"Fiona I'm sorry but there is no way that you can be Simon's biological mother."

She sat in a stilled silence, as though in a

trance attempting to take in his words, numbed by the shock.

Her husband broke the silence." That's ridiculous. Of course she's his mother; the samples must somehow have got mixed up with someone else's."

"The laboratory methods and procedures would make that an impossibility. I'm sorry to say Fiona that I can only assume that your child must somehow have accidentally been switched at birth in the hospital."

The statement snapped Fiona from her shell shocked state " Of course Simon's my child; I had him at home. I never left his side for months; Simon is my child."

Fiona saw the incomprehension appear in deep ripples across the specialist's forehead. "I really can't explain it."

"There is only one explanation" retorted Dave. "The laboratory, regardless of their methods and procedures have somehow messed up."

"Fiona I can only suggest after the uncertainty of the DNA results taken from your blood that we take another sample for analysis;

this time a mouth swab. I apologise and assure you that we will get to the bottom of this."

After Fiona's sample was taken the DCI let his feelings be known and then took his wife home.

After talking well into the night they finally went to bed, neither one falling asleep, both still in thought;Fiona remembering Simons birth, her husband puzzling death. *If It's possible for a slip up at the laboratory then maybe that's what's happened with one of our suspects original specimen.*

The following day Jack Green was brought back into the station and when his solicitor arrived he remonstrated with D.S. Smith.

"Mr. Jeffries we haven't brought your client back in for questioning, we require another DNA sample."

Green's eyes met his solicitors." Officer, you have my clients DNA type on your data base. Why would you need another one? I find this highly irregular and I advise Mr. Green not to give one."

"Mr. Jeffries, because this is regarding a new

crime, away from his original crime for which his earlier specimen was taken, he cannot refuse us one if we arrest him under suspicion, but I would prefer for him to volunteer one."

His solicitor was angry but powerless and a hair and saliva sample were taken before he was allowed to go.

Tony Jack was re-interviewed and asked for a second DNA sample, and upon refusal the D.S. threatened to get one through the courts, whereupon Jack gave one voluntarily.

Robinson was brought in, arriving just before his solicitor.

D.S. Derek Smith once again headed the interview.

"Mr. Grant we require a further DNA sample from your client."

"But he's already provided you with one."

" Yes he has already submitted one so what harm could a second one do?"

"I don't know what game you're playing Detective Sergeant Smith but I'm not happy with it and won't allow it. After giving you one voluntarily, there are no legal grounds to demand a second one."

"You leave me no option; we will obtain permission through the courts." he said angrily as he gave the order to release Robinson.

Two days later Jack Green's and Tony Jack's results came back, identical to the ones on the data base. Arnold could only shake his head in frustration. "Okay, then the mix-up has to be with Robinson's sample".

Harry Turner watched Arnold walk out through the main doors and shook his head, a look of disgust on his face. Turner wanted as much as anyone for the murderer to be found but also revelled in the fact that apart from Stamp, Arnold was getting nowhere fast. "He's clueless.

He's convinced the other murderer is either Green, Jack or Robinson. Why not charge them all inspector?" he sarcastically quipped to his colleagues.

"Harry it's hard enough without any in-fighting" said Scott, one of the team.

"But the man's determined to land somebody; anybody. Okay on the face of it all three suspects fit the bill in every department except for the DNA. What if Stamp's accomplice isn't any one of them.There's got to be others out there that tick all the right boxes, including, I think the DNA box. Arnold's determined to get one of the suspects in the frame and I don't think he's bothered which one. I think it's more about him than whoever's guilty. He said he guarantees that it's one of them but the last murder took place while they were all under twenty four hour surveillance. I don't think it's any of them; Arnold really scares me."

CHAPTER TWENTY-TWO

"Detective Chief Inspector, your application for a further DNA sample from your suspect Mr. Robinson somewhat baffles me. Why would you require a further sample when he has already volunteered one which remains on the data base?"

"Your Honour, it appears that a possible mix up of samples may originally have occurred in the laboratory and the only way to be certain is for a retest."

"I think we are treading dangerous ground here. Since the introduction of DNA evidence many criminals have been brought to justice, its infallibility beyond question. You now say that it's a possibility that analysed specimens can be mistakenly attributed. I find that alarming. We have to be certain in every case that results are beyond doubt or we could be opening up a rather large can of worms, let alone create confusion in the general public's perception of how safe DNA evidence really is."

"Your honour I realise this is regrettable and I am certain that I will never find myself in this position again. I understand the importance of maintaining the integrity of DNA evidence. Having said that, with the severity of the crimes in question, and my not being convinced of the suspects innocence, a further sample would either incriminate or clear him."

"Detective Chief Inspector a suspect is normally only legally bound to provide one DNA sample but circumstances may arise where that could be questioned. Before allowing a second DNA sample, I need to be assured in my own mind that the laboratory findings of the sample would return proof of the suspects connection to the crime in question. You cannot give me an assurance that would be the case, so in allowing a further sample to be taken without producing that proof would not serve the purpose of justice. I have to balance probability against improbability. Also what concerns me in this particular application is your statement of not being convinced of your suspects innocence, rather than being convinced of his guilt. You are not in possession of any other compelling evidence regarding this individual and in the absence of it I refuse the application and remind you that any person is innocent until proven guilty; not the other way around."

The D.C.I thanked the judge for his time and walked out of the chambers, fuming inside.

Arnold was sat at home in the semi-darkness, the curtains open as shadows danced across his long living room Wall. He never saw one of them, his mind in another place. He had convinced himself of Robinson's guilt and was still angry at the judge's refusal of the application. *How can I get another DNA sample from him?* The question kept burning in his mind without answer. Eventually he closed the curtains and climbed the stairs still cursing. He lay next to Fiona staring at the ceiling, wishing some divine intervention would appear with the answer. His eyes closed, his mind relaxed and he was headed for a long deserved deep sleep when he suddenly shot up. "That's it! That's the answer. Bring him in on a trumped up charge and we can legally start the whole DNA process back up again."

Fiona stirred. "Was you saying something Dave?"

"You're dreaming Fiona. Go back to sleep." His mind was alive with ideas and he got very little sleep, something he needed more than he realised.

The following day around noon Arnold left the office and drove to a housing estate where Robinson lived. It was renowned for trouble. He pulled up outside a shabby looking house with overgrown hedges and walked to the front door. Before he had the time to knock, the door was opened by an unkempt individual whose sour body odour, mixed in with a stale alcohol stench that appeared had long impregnated his clothes. He half pulled the inspector into the house as he quickly glanced around making certain that no-one saw his arrival. "What are you doing here?If anyone sees us talking I'm dead; you never come here; you know that."

"Johnny relax, you're overreacting. I thought I'd pay you a visit, after all you haven't visited me for several months. The deal was for you to feed me information, keeping me up to date with what's going down, and I look after you in return; a bit of cash here and there and occasionally turn a blind eye when you go astray. It's been one-sided recently but luckily for you I've found a way for you to make it up to me. I want you to come into the station to report an assault. Do you know a guy called Mike Robinson?"

Arnold showed him a photograph. Johnny shook his head.

"He lives two streets away from yourself. You're to come in and say you're convinced he's the man who assaulted you."

"Hang on a minute. What's happening here? I thought when you first mentioned it you wanted me to witness an assault, not myself getting done over, especially when he lives round here. I'm not doing that, I'll get a good kicking if I'm lucky."

"Johnny, like I said earlier, relax. Robinson isn't a bad apple. He's straight as a die. He's got no form and keeps out of trouble."

"Why are you setting him up then?"

"I'm not exactly setting him up. He's a

witness to a minor crime but he won't play ball by testifying. I only want him leant on so that I can have a heart to heart with him. The day after I talk to him, I'll ring you to let you know and you contact the station to say you're not now convinced that it was him, and he's off the hook. He'll never know it was you and he won't set eyes on you."

"I'm not sure."

"I am Johnny. You owe me. Do this favour and we're all square. If you don't, I think you're forgetting a couple of things that I've got over you." Johnny nodded and agreed to do it.

Arnold took ten pounds from his wallet." Get a deodoriser for the room and a bar of soap for yourself."

He came away pleased with the result. All he had to do was sit and wait knowing when the results from Robinson's new DNA sample came through they would have their serial killer.

Later that day John Black turned up at Coventry Central police station to report the assault. Harry Turner was talking to a colleague in the lobby and half heard the complaint to the duty desk officer. When he heard Robinson's name and address given across he stopped mid-conversation, concentrating solely on Black's complaint as he moved across to the desk. Black's face was familiar but he couldn't place it.

"The idiot, all the trouble Robinson's in and he can't even stay out of a fight. Where did it happen?"

Black looked apprehensively towards Turner who immediately knew something was amiss. "He came at me along the main road, across from where I live."

"Did you provoke him?"

"No. I've only seen him a couple of times. I live around the corner from him and that's how I knew where he lived."

An hour later Robinson was back in custody and after being interviewed with his solicitor present D.S. Scott Andrews asked him for a DNA sample as Arnold had told him to do.

"You've got one. I won't give you another!" he snapped angrily. "I shouldn't even be here. It's a set-up" he said, looking towards his solicitor.

"You are obsessed with obtaining a further

DNA specimen from my client after being refused one from him on my advice and being denied one by the court, quite rightly throwing out your application. I can't believe you are even requesting one. The answer's still no."

"Mr. Grant, because it's the start of a new investigation relating to a separate offence we can legally extract one with or without his or your permission."

"But I don't want to give another one."

What are you frightened of? thought Arnold as he watched the interview on screen, an inward feeling of self satisfaction emerging.

"The police are unfortunately within their rights Mr. Robinson but I find this whole episode too convenient by far. I will get to the bottom of it and also complain to your Chief Superintendent about your methods Detective Sergeant Andrews."

A second mouth swab was taken and a hair removed from Robinson head.

CHAPTER TWENTY-THREE

Arnold had his team together discussing ways forward on the murder cases when he informed them that Robinson had given a second DNA sample after being accused of assault and that the results would soon be with them. Harry Turner watched the D.C.I. but never heard a word he said. His mind was somewhere else trying to work out what game Arnold was playing. Then he remembered where he had seen John Black before. He recalled that years earlier Black had been a police informant on several occasions. He also recollected Black getting off a burglary charge that he shouldn't have done.

When the meeting was over Turner looked at Black's police file to discover it was Arnold who had the burglary charge dropped.

After dark, Harry Turner visited Black's house and once again on opening the door he hurried the detective through. "What is it with you lot? I don't see anyone for months; the next thing you're all at my door."

"And who else has visited you?"

Black stood in silence. He knew he'd slipped up.

"I'll ask you once again. Who came to see you?"

Black bit his lip shaking his head.

"If you don't come clean I'll arrest you for obstruction. You've nothing to fear. Just tell me."

"Are you lot batting for the same team? I was asked to do a favour regarding Robinson so he would stand up in court as a witness. Now you're here as if you know nothing about it."

"Mike Robinson is a suspect in a very serious crime although it appears that he is most likely innocent."

"He told me I'd nothing to fear, that Robinson was totally harmless and had no form."

"Who told you?"

Black looked at the detective trying to

understand it all.

"I'll ask again. Who told you.? You're life could have been put in danger if Robinson was guilty."

"The bastard. Dave Arnold; he came round. He's set me up. I can't believe it with all the information I've given to him."

"So you're still working as an informant."

"Here and there. I keep my ear to the ground."

"And what do you get in return?"

"Come on you know how it works, but I don't get it. If Arnold wasn't putting pressure on him to act as a witness, what did he gain from it?, especially as he was going to ring me at some point to inform the police that I might have been mistaken after all."

"I know what he got from it. You don't need to know but if I were you I'd visit someone out of town for a couple of months while the dust settles. It's going to get very hot and sticky around here. Is there somewhere you can lay low for a while?"

"Give me three hours. I'll be off with all my belongings to a mate in Scotland and I'm staying there".

Turner climbed into his car and reached into his jacket pocket. He pulled out a dictaphone and replayed the tape. A smile appeared briefly on his face. He had waited a long time for this.

Back at his home, after erasing his own voice from the recording he replayed the tape to make certain that Black's answers alone were enough to incriminate Arnold and then anonymously sent a copy of the tape to Robinson's solicitor.

The DNA results came back from the laboratory. "Damn! I was certain that Robinson's DNA had got mixed up. We're back to square one again; a third accomplice at large to any one of Green, Jack or Robinson." Arnold shook his head. "The investigation's going backwards."

The next morning Chief Superintendent Burns walked into the incident room to announce, without detail that Detective Chief Inspector Arnold had been taken off the inquiry and was suspended from duty until an internal investigation had taken place. The team looked on perplexed, but before anyone could ask any questions the Chief super asked Harry Turner to come to his office.

"From this moment in time we need someone else to lead the inquiry. Harry I want you to take over from Dave."

"I'll only be too glad to but what's happened? Why has Dave been suspended?"

"I won't go into too much detail but what I do tell you doesn't go out of this office; understood?"

Harry Turner nodded, a convincing puzzled look across his face.

"D.C.I Arnold for some reason believed Robinson's original DNA sample to have gotten mixed up in the laboratory and being unable through the courts to secure a second specimen obtained one by illegal means. That's as much as I'm prepared to say for now."

"Personally speaking sir, Dave Arnold had totally convinced himself that one of either Green, Jack or Robinson was the other killer, regardless of the fact that all three were under twenty four hour surveillance before the murder of Edmunds. I think he was putting too much emphasis on them which slowed down the search in any other direction. The main factor behind his thinking was the discovery of them all owning a Fiat Punto with tinted rear windows. There must be many more out there, and I would like to appeal again for them through the media."

"Do it. Hopefully it will give us some new leads, It's a good job we've got Stamp already or the shit would really hit the fan upstairs with Arnolds antics. Robinson's solicitor is making an official complaint against us for his stupidity. It makes us all look corrupt."

A call came through to Arnolds office. "Acting D.C.I. Harry Turner here. Can I help?"

"Good morning inspector I'm Doctor Hilton specialising in psychiatry. I may possibly have information on the series of murders that have recently occurred in the Midlands area."

"What kind of information Doctor?"

"It's in too much detail to discuss over the telephone but if you could come to my office on Arrow Street in an hour's time I will be clear of clients by then."

An hour later the acting D.C.I.

Accompanied by Jane Morgan were shown into the psychiatrist's office.

Turner shook the doctors hand before introducing Jane. "Doctor thanks for contacting us. I was intrigued by your call. Exactly what kind of information do you have?"

"I obviously have a professional interest in activity such as the murders. I try to spot any pattern that might emerge. Not that I'm aware of one, but when I heard the name of the murdered strip club owner it seemed familiar. I tried to recall where I'd heard it before and it dawned on me over breakfast this morning. A client I saw years ago had mentioned that particular individual as being a part of her problem. When I arrived at the office I took out her file. Sharon Peterson. She had numerous personal problems that culminated in depression and several suicide attempts. She was admitted to Springvale Mental Health Centre for assessment. That's where I first came into contact with her. Sharon actually lived within the unit for nearly a year. She regained the confidence to live back in the community over five years ago, and continued with regular counselling until the poor girl was killed in a road accident. That's the only reason that I felt able to divulge the information without any confidentiality issues, especially as she had no known relatives. While going over Sharon's file I jotted down other people's names she had accused of playing a part in her downfall, and then cross checked those with back issues of the newspapers to see if there was any further connection to any of the other murders. Inspector, I don't understand, with Sharon being dead for all this time, but she named Farrell, the vile photographer; her words, as being her worst nightmare. She also spoke of Shaun Dixon being her pimp who was introduced to her by a drug dealer who supplied her and lived in Coventry, although she never mentioned his name. This cannot just be coincidence."

"Doctor Hilton I really appreciate you contacting us. This information is vital, please could you give us her last known address?"

"She said she was regarded as homeless, only staying with a friend but was looking for her own place, so we didn't actually have an address for her."

"Homeless? What about her husband?"

"Husband? Sharon was never married. She did live with someone for two years before she was admitted to Springvale though. Her partner was a woman; Sharon was bi-sexual."

This information visibly shook the inspector. "Are you absolutely certain she wasn't married?"

"I'm in no doubt whatsoever."

Turner asked "Would you have Sharon's partner's details on file?"

"The only thing I can tell you is that her first name was Chris. I'm not even aware of her surname. She only visited Sharon once, and Sharon never had any other visitor in her time at Springvale. I can tell you that it was her partner finishing the relationship that took Sharon over the edge to attempt suicide again. Everything that happened throughout her life made her deeply depressive not helped by the drugs she was addicted to. She couldn't cope with the relationship ending."

"Would you possibly have a photograph on file? one that we could show to her old neighbours, once we have her address."

"Sorry there isn't one", he replied shaking his head.

"Doctor your help has been invaluable; if anything else comes to mind please get in touch."

Outside, sat in the parked car Turner scratched his head. "This is a real breakthrough but what I fail to understand is why the clues we were sent, obviously from the real killer, saying that she was his wife, because after all she was the reason for the revenge attacks. Plus it would coincide with when Sharon lived with the other woman. I don't get it."

"Also why wait all that time before taking his revenge?" added Jane. "Was he in some way restricted?,confined? We should check all recent releases from prisons and mental health units".

D.I. Turner asked "Could Sharon have fooled the doctor into thinking she was having a relationship with another woman when she was really married?"

"Why would she? Sharon attended the sessions of counselling voluntarily after she left the assessment unit. She wanted further help and I'm sure she would have only told the truth. If she had been lying, the doctor would have spotted it straight away. Don't forget she was manipulated by men and had no problem giving all their names to the doctor. If she had been married and her husband had been as bad as the others she would have given the doctor his name. On the other hand if he had been a good man towards her, she would have offered his name, being the only positive in her life. No, Sharon was definitely not married regardless of the misleading clues."

"Then what are we to make of the clues? With what you said before Jane regarding the possibility of a relative or friend assisting in the murders, I think we'll run Sharon's name past Stamp, Robinson, Jack and Green to try and establish if there's a link."

Stamp was re-interviewed first. He sat stern faced alongside his solicitor as the questioning began.

"Information has come to light regarding the name of the person who these murders are based upon. Sharon Peterson. What's your link to her?"

Stamp's face changed into a puzzled expression the name having thrown him completely off his stride,playing her name over and over again in his mind, trying to make sense of it. "It can't be, can it?"

"Who is Sharon Peterson" asked Turner?

"How old is she?"

"Why would her age matter?", his heart upping a beat, realising Stamp knew her.

"I had a step daughter of that name. I kicked -----; she left home at sixteen. I've never heard of or seen Sharon since then, over ten years ago. What has she to do with all of this?"

"You haven't seen her for all that time? Mr. Stamp, I find that impossible to believe. You are killing people because of her."

"I keep telling you I've killed no-one, nor was my car down any damn lane. I don't know what's happening here but I promise you I haven't seen Sharon since the day she left."

"Would you have any photographs of Sharon?"

"I got rid of all her mother's possessions years ago apart from several photo's of Joyce. Her daughter isn't on any of them."

"I have to inform you that Sharon Peterson was killed in an accident approximately four years ago."

Stamp sighed momentarily, putting his hand to his mouth which could have been mistaken for shock and grief but was in reality a sharp pang of guilt, which he quickly overcame. "So why are the murders centred around her if she died all that time ago?"

"You tell us. You're one of the killers."

Stamp never responded.

"You said you live alone. What's the address of Sharon's mother."

"Joyce died two years after Sharon went."

"Did she ever contact her mother after she left?"

"There was no contact whatsoever. I'm not even sure if she knew her mother was dead."

"I want a list of addresses of all Sharon's friends and relatives that you can recall."

"There's only one aunt that I know of, Joyce's sister. She lives somewhere in Bradford. Her address is in my telephone book at home, that is if she still lives there. She never made contact after Joyce died although I left numerous messages on her answer phone and wrote several letters to her without reply. She could tell you more about Sharon and who her friends were."

"Mr. Popular aren't you? Nobody seems to want to know you; I wonder why?"

After the interview was terminated, Turner and Jane Morgan talked about the relationship that had been uncovered. "Do you believe any of it Jane?, that he'd never laid eyes on her since she moved out; I mean the letters from his supposed unknown accomplice; plus all the indisputable overwhelming evidence stacked up against him."

"I know exactly what you mean, although if you're honest with yourself, you aren't really asking my opinion, only casting slight doubt upon your own."

Turner smiled at her. "You're too damn good. That's why Arnold got you on the team. No! he's guilty alright, but there's more to it. It isn't that straightforward. It's there before us but we can't see it, although when we checked his story out regarding his number plates with the graphic design shop it appeared he was telling the truth unless it could have been forethought to have an alibi in waiting."

"But if he went to that extreme, why not just fix false registration plates to start with." added Jane.

Turner looked straight through Jane as he rubbed his chin, pondering. "The problem I've got is that I actually think he may be telling the truth about not seeing Sharon for a long time, and I'm convinced he didn't know she was dead making it at least four years since he's seen her or had contact with her so why would he kill on her behalf as a stepfather assisting the murderer. He would have to know she was dead. I can't quite grasp it."

"Either that or he's one of the best liars I've ever come across" Jane commented.

Sharon's aunt was contacted and the few relatives of Sharon were questioned without any of them knowing of her demise, having had no word of her since she was sixteen. No one had a photograph of Sharon. The names of two close friends that she had, emerged, and after tracing them through old school records they were located. Unfortunately there was no school photograph of different classes, only printed information. Turner and D.S. Derek Smith drove through to Norwich after arranging a meeting with Anne Preston, one of Sharon's friends.

After the introductions Turner asked the questions. "Anne when did you last see Sharon Peterson?"

"I haven't seen her for years. She stayed at my house for six months after her stepfather threw her out on her sixteenth birthday. She tried contacting her mother but both the landline and mobile numbers were changed. It would have been him. He was horrible towards Sharon. He used to hit her, and her mother got it as well if she interfered."

"Do you know of her last address?"

"I don't, but Chris might know."

"Would that be Chris Brown?"

"Yes. All three of us were friends at school, but Sharon and Chris were very close and they socialised a lot aged about seventeen or eighteen. I can give you her address."

"Would you have any photo's of Sharon?"

"I'm afraid I don't have any."

Back in the car Turner checked for Chris Brown's landline number to make certain she would be at home and arranged to see her in Peterborough before going back to Coventry. Before starting the car Turner was in deep thought. "It appears that Stamp had no love for Sharon throwing her out of the family home, and she would have most likely hated him, which makes it even more baffling as to why Stamp would kill on her behalf."

"An underlying guilt coming to the surface knowing his actions could have led her into prostitution." replied Smith.

"A possibility, but if that were to be true, once again he would have to be lying about not seeing Sharon for a long time and I don't think he was lying about that."

The police arrived at Chris Brown's address and were greeted by a short haired stocky woman.

"Good morning. I'm Acting Detective Chief Inspector Turner and this is Detective Sergeant Smith. I rang through a while ago. Would you be

Christine Brown?"

"No, that's my partner. You'd better come in."
They were both ushered through.

"I'm D.I. Turner and this is D.S. Smith. Chris, do you know of a woman by the name of Sharon Peterson?"

"Sharon. Yes we were friends since school, but I haven't seen her in years. She's okay isn't she?"

"Unfortunately she died in a road accident approximately four years ago."

"Oh my God! Poor Sharon. I saw on the news where her stepfather had been arrested for murder. I couldn't believe it. Sharon and I were really close once. We lived together but her drugs took over everything and ended up destroying what we had. I came home from work one night and both the gas and electricity had been cut off. Sharon had supposedly been paying all the bills with the money I gave her every week as my share of the housekeeping. She'd spent the lot on heroin. I couldn't believe I had been so stupid. A few days later, when I got home from work she was on the doorstep crying and begging me to forgive her. The bailiffs had been and taken virtually everything from the house. She had hidden all the court correspondence and said nothing. It was the last straw and I threw her out."

"Was that the last time you saw her?"

"No. I saw her once more, at the hospital after she tried to kill herself. She'd had a shit life, she was kicked out when she left school and her life went even further downhill from that point on."

"Was she, to your knowledge, at any time a prostitute?"

Chris looked to her partner. "Sorry Sue, I know I told you most things about Sharon." Chris turned back to D.I. Turner. "Yes she was; Too dependant upon the drugs. She worked the streets while we were together. I hated it and tried to help her stop both working the street and the drugs but it was useless, she was too far in. It's sad that she's dead but I honestly expected that the drugs would have got her in the end. But why all the questions now if she died four years ago?"

"It's part of an ongoing investigation regarding a male friend that she knew quite well."

"Jack!" stated Chris.

"Would that be Tony Jack or Jack Green?"

"I'm really not sure. She only referred to him as Jack and I presumed it was a Christian name but I could have been wrong. I never met him but he was the only man she ever trusted. He was madly in love with her and he used to tell her often, even though he knew she was with me and although she was working the streets when they met, they never had sex once; she told him it would destroy their friendship. He gave her more money than the punters, any time she asked for it. If he had it, she got it. Sharon thought he was a mug, although she liked his company In small doses, someone to pour her heart out to knowing full well she'd be covered in sympathy."

"Did she tell you where he lived?"

"It's strange when I think back, for as much as she talked about him, nothing really emerged about his background, as I said I'm not even certain if Jack was a Christian name or a surname and she never mentioned his address. The little money he had was the main reason she allowed him to hang around her; she'd bleed him dry if it was quiet on the street, and still take his money when she had plenty of punters. He was her reserve heroin account holder, as she described him to me, while laughing. Even though I never knew him I still felt sorry for him. She really just led him on enough to keep his interest. Anybody as far gone on drugs as Sharon was would rob their own mother for a fix; he was a walk in the park, a kind of sugar daddy without having to give him a sweetener. Occasionally they would go out for a meal and have long conversations and I knew that Jack, like myself tried to help her come off the street and off the heroin, but it was no good. I know they never slept together; she would have told me, it wouldn't have been a problem, but as much as she liked putting the world to rights with him, Sharon couldn't stand being in his company for longer than a few hours at a time. She said he became a bit of a weirdo, saying and doing strange things and then, when he was in another room she used to hear him talking to himself. She often found him setting the cutlery on his table, only to look at it and then swap it all around, again and again and again as if in some sort of strange compulsive manner. She knew by things that he did that he had mental issues, but I personally think that was their true bond, not that Sharon was crazy but all their problems in life had been because of bad parents who never gave a shit about either one of them. Sharon told me all about his upbringing"

"You say you never met him, but did you ever see him? We could show you some photographs of who it could possibly be."

"I never saw him at any time. At first I even doubted his existence."

"Would you have any photo's of Sharon?"

"I did have but Sue and I decided to cut all ties with the past and so we threw out all the photo's of Sue's ex, and all those of Sharon over two years ago."

"You're quite sure that she never had any other men friends, possibly someone she might have tried to keep a secret?"

"Definitely not; I would have known because we had an entirely open relationship without the need for secrets. Apart from Jack, whoever he might have been, Sharon never trusted any other man. When I visited her at the hospital after she tried to commit suicide she told me she would be living at an assessment unit for a while and later she would move in with Jack, although she stressed to me that it was on condition they still never slept together to keep their friendship intact. He would have taken her straight in. She liked him a lot in a strange way but she admitted he also made her skin crawl. She also confessed that It wasn't an ideal arrangement and she would have preferred not to move in, but with his cash and her with none, she was still going to rip him off. I decided then, as she would be looked after, not to visit again. I've never seen or heard of her since, until you knocked at the door. What is it that Jack's done; it must be bad if you've taken the time to track me down which couldn't have been easy."

"It's part of an ongoing investigation, so I can't really say. I would appreciate it if we could send someone round to see you to try and build a likeness up on computer of Sharon, and thank you for talking to us. If you remember any other detail no matter how small you feel it might be, please contact us straight away as it could be very helpful."

"Ricky there is only one more person left before Karina's being avenged is complete but I cannot locate him. I've tried everything, short of visiting Brighton where he used to live. I've spent days researching records and files and in the libraries archives; nothing. He must be found. I will not be able to rest until he is. Hardy had always worked as a baker and I've decided to go to Brighton to see if I can find him."

CHAPTER TWENTY-FOUR

Gregor Natas took the book from his drawer and opened it to reveal a photograph of James, and thought back on the good times they shared. "It is time" he said determinedly in his Eastern European accent. They will all pay."

He drove out to his aunt's farmhouse and let himself in, holding his nose to evade the pungent smell emitting from the living room, which he avoided entering; no desire to see the extent of her badly decomposing body as she sat in her armchair, not having been moved at all by Gregor once he had lifted the pillow from her face. He had cried at her feeble attempts to breathe. Gregor had told her of his intentions to avenge James but with his aunt's threats of calling the police, she could not be allowed to stand in his way.

The old house had a large secure and soundproof cellar and behind the wine racks stood a semicircle of three heavy wooden chairs, all facing a fourth freestanding chair. Gregor had fastened the other three securely to the concrete floor. He had cut away a large percentage of each seat in the middle and attached handcuffs to both arms of each chair and affixed chains to both front chair legs. He went out to his van and brought in supplies of bottled water and tinned ham before he climbed back into his van and stared at the farmhouse.

"No-one should have to feel the agony that both his mother and I did. I love you Julie; one day you will forgive me."

Gregor waited, parked in his white van complete with false number plates, outside a large detached house in an expensive suburb of Leeds. All had large gardens which was the reason for the false advertisement on the side of the van so as not to look out of place; TOM SIMS. LANDSCAPE GARDENER. The sign in green vinyl on a magnetic strip, also included a false phone number. He had two signs made up for him at different graphic designers, one reading; ALAN GARDENER. M.O.T. The other read; SMITH and PASCALL BUILDERS, followed by another false

225

mobile number. He had cut out the lettering and numbering from both vinyl's to make up his sign.

Any possible future CCTV footage appearing on television would not be recognised by the designers, and in his disguise, he would not be identified.

He waited. Eventually the heavy electrically operated wrought iron gates rolled slowly open before Judge Bowers drove his Jaguar out onto the road. Gregor instantly recognised him from when he sat in the Law courts ten years earlier, attending the trial of James' killer.

Gregor, on seeing the news coverage on local television had cried out James' name determined to right this wrong. Judge Bowers, Graeme Railton, the solicitor and Stamford, the wrongly sentenced killer would to be brought to the court of Gregor Natas' to face their trial.

Gregor kept a daily watch on the judge for over a week alternating between his van and another car.

Bowers as usual, pulled into the multi-story city centre car park, and reversed into his reserved car parking space. Gregor was parked next to it, pretending to take out something from the back. As the Judge passed by, Gregor roughly grabbed the judges face clamping the chloroform soaked cloth in position, firmly over his mouth and nose. The Judges reaction was to fight free but Gregor was too strong, and within seconds, weakened, he fell limply into his abductors arms.

Several minutes later the van pulled out of the car park, Judge Bowers laid over the discarded vinyl signs in the back. In a quiet area, about a mile out of the city centre, Gregor removed the false number plates before continuing the long journey through to his aunts farm house.

Two hours later he drove into his aunt Julies drive, having had one stop to give a second dose of chloroform to the judge. Opening the back door and cellar door, Gregor eased the judge over his shoulders and carried him down into the cellar.

The Judge came around an hour later, disorientated. His senses snapped back into reality as he was unable to move his hands, handcuffed to the chair arms. He could only move his legs a couple of inches; chains tight around his bare ankles. His trousers and shorts had been removed. Fear engulfed him, unable to shout out, his mouth stuck in place with the strong tape that covered it. Unknown to him, even without his gag, shouting would have served no purpose. The cellar walls were thick and the door he was unaware of would absorb any sound. The intense blackness allowed nothing to be visible. He sat in forced stillness amid increasing panic throughout the day.

Gregor sat in his car, again with false number plates, in a parking bay across from Sedgebrook and Railton's Solicitors' office in Oxford. At four o'clock Graeme Railton emerged through the main entrance and walked towards the multi storey car park several streets away. As he drove out onto the main road Gregor followed, two cars behind. Fifteen minutes later, at the edge of a housing estate Railton drove into the deserted car park of the Eagle Pub. Gregor, driving past, pulled up to see Railton entering the pub.

After an hour Gregor left his car and walked around the outside of the pub peering through the windows into the various empty bars. He saw Railton sat by himself drinking what appeared to be a large glass of whisky. Gregor returned to his car and waited for the solicitor to emerge.

At seven o'clock exactly a taxi pulled into the car park and the horn sounded.

Five minutes later Railton came staggering out and climbed in. *Just short of three hours drinking and he's nearly falling over. He must really have been putting the drink away.*

He followed the taxi until it entered a small exclusive housing estate dropping him off at a large detached house. "Bought by clients rich enough to hire him, with his knowledge of legal loop-holes. He was able to get the guilty off by either cleverly misrepresenting the true facts, or by recognising a technicality or let out." Gregor angrily muttered to himself as the lights were turned on.

Gregor waited close to Railton's house until late evening without anyone entering or leaving before he drove through to his aunts farmhouse.

Bowers heard the cellar door opening. The strong spotlights were switched on aimed directly at the chairs as the judges eyes screwed up in pain, the long hours of darkness instantly turning to brilliance. It would have had him screaming in agony but for the tape gagging him. Slowly he unscrewed his eyes, as they adjusted to the light and looked directly at Gregor, not knowing him, uncertain of what was to happen to him.

Gregor walked over to the wall across from the Judge and hung a large clock upon it that showed the seconds as they ticked away. He strode up to the Judges chair and bent down at its side as Bowers eyes fearfully followed him. Gregor removed a large plastic bowl from beneath the chair that was his toilet, and without looking at the Judge walked across the cellar to empty it. When he returned, deliberately avoiding Bowers eye contact, he replaced the bowl and moved across to a refrigerator from which he took a sandwich and a plastic bottle of water. He stared directly at the judge. "I am going to remove your tape for three minutes so that you can eat and drink. After that time it will be replaced whether you have eaten or not, so time is all important. I will not answer any questions, nor will I talk once I have removed the tape so use your time only for eating and drinking."

As soon as the gag was removed the

questions started. "What the hell's happening? Who are you? What am I doing here?"

Gregor held the sandwich before his mouth in a pair of tongs as he turned in silence and pointed towards the clock.

"What the hell's happening? Why have you taken me captive?" the Judge repeated, although the second time of asking was more through desperation rather than anger. Gregor again pointed to the clock which showed only two minutes remained. Needing answers to his questions but needing to eat and drink more, he stretched his head forward toward the tongs and bit into the sandwich. Hungrily, he ate the first mouthful as he looked at the clock, then to Gregor and again back to the clock as he took another bite from the food, chewing frantically, staring at his captor, knowing that for now he would get no answers. He swallowed, immediately thrusting his head forward once again, desperate for more, as Gregor pointed to the time with only thirty seconds remaining. He put the tongs down with over half the sandwich still intact and unscrewed the top from the water bottle, putting it to the judges lips. He drank several mouthfuls before it was pulled away from him, the time elapsed.

"For Gods sake man. What's happening? Why am I here?"

Without answering Gregor held a fresh piece of tape moving it towards the judges mouth. He shook his head back and forth giving the message out that he was not prepared to be gagged again. "I won't ask any questions and I'll remain quiet. Please don't put it back on." Gregor tried to administer the tape again, only for the Judge to shake his head from side to side. Without a word he put the tape down and moved across to a worktop out of view, returning with a bottle and cloth, the label on the bottle clearly marked chloroform, holding it in front of the Judge. Confronted with the alternative he nodded in a resigned manner. "Okay, I won't struggle. You can put it back on."

Gregor turned out the light and left the Judge alone with his darkness.

At seven thirty a.m. he was parked close to Railton's house and waited until eight thirty when a taxi from the same company pulled into his drive. Gregor took notes. Eight thirty a.m.

taxi firm 372--372, its bright yellow signs on both front doors. Railton climbed in and Gregor followed before the taxi dropped him back off at the Eagle public house where he got into his own car and drove to the multi-storey car park close to his office.

Gregor checked Railton's name in the phone directory against his address and during the course of the day rang it fifteen times to check if anyone came or went. It was never answered.

When the solicitor had finished work, he once again drove to the Eagle pub, coming out drunk again at seven o'clock to climb into a different taxi from the same company. After following them home, Gregor drove back to his aunt's farmhouse after removing his false number plates.

The Judge sat rigidly as he walked in, the heavy door creaking its way open. Gregor tended to Bowers waste bowl without speaking before walking across to the fridge and taking out another sandwich and bottle of water. Stood in front of Bower whose eyes were once again screwed tight with the light's brilliance, Gregor turned to point to the clock "three minutes only." He stripped the tape from the Judges mouth and offered the sandwich once again held by the tongs. Bowers ate furiously, desperate to finish before the clock could beat him, his hunger extreme. After his fill of water, assisted by Gregor, the new tape was brought towards his face, only able to blurt out one sentence.

"Please let my family know that I'm alright. Put them out of their miser----"

The tape back in position, Gregor turned out the light, locked the door behind him and left.

Parked inconspicuously, a mile away from Railton's house, Gregor set the alarm on his mobile for eight o'clock, reclined his driver's seat and fell to sleep.

"Eight thirty a.m. Bang on time." The taxi bearing 372--372 pulled into Railton's drive to take him to pick his car up from the Eagle car park.

As Gregor Natas waited for Railton to finish work, he listened to the news. Deep concern was expressed by the family of the missing Judge from Leeds. Railton came out at his usual time, driving once again to the Eagle public house. Twenty minutes before Gregor felt the taxi would be sent, he rang the office to cancel the car for Railton and then attached his own 372--372 door stickers he'd had made in the morning; drove to the bar door and waited for the solicitor to emerge. The landlord came out and beckoned Gregor over to the door to help with Railton. He had managed to struggle outside with him but couldn't get any further without assistance. Railton was so drunk he was incapable of walking, so Gregor, apprehensive of facing the landlord, wondered that with one of the main outside lights not working, that the landlord wouldn't be able to get a view of him, and disguised as he was, went to help.

With difficulty they both managed to get him in the back of the car where he immediately fell into a drunken sleep. As Gregor drove away he thought to himself that it would not be easy getting his huge frame from the car to the cellar at his aunt's house. At the edge of the large dark car park Gregor administered the chloroform with ease, after making certain there were no CCTV cameras erected.

When they arrived, Gregor left Railton's heavy, inert body laid across the back seat, first going into the cellar as Bowers screwed his eyes again at the rush of brilliant light and before he could adjust to the light, Gregor, in a swift movement had pulled a snug fitting beanie over Bower's head before he could react. It came to the bottom of his nose totally blindfolding him.

Gregor then went to the shed and took a wheel barrow across to his car where, with difficulty he loaded Railton's body into it and after struggling for half an hour, Railton was chained to the seat next to the Judge, another hat over Railton's head and eyes. Without his wrists being handcuffed or chains around his ankles, Railton, slumped in his seat, would have slithered to the floor.

Gregor stopped himself as he was about to gag Railton. Because of his drunken condition coupled with the chloroform, he feared that he may be sick even though he had travelled through okay; the last thing he wanted was for Railton to die, choking on his own vomit before he could face trial. He decided it was of more importance that his intended defendants weren't able to recognise each other until the day of their trial as he wanted to see the disbelief and fear on each of their faces. So if Railton died on his own vomit, so be it; it was a price he would accept.

Gregor removed Bower's blindfold and tape.

Immediately he tried to look across to where all the noise had been coming from, frozen by shock, moving only his eyes, scouring up and down the lifeless looking body whose position on the chair was only maintained by the tethering. "Oh my God, you've killed him."

Without answer a sandwich was thrust towards his face in the tongs. Gregor poked him on the shoulder and pointed to the clock whereby Bowers, as if by habit chewed quickly away, without taking his eyes off Railton's body. After drinking his water he begged for answers. All that was forthcoming was new tape across his mouth and his beanie placed once again over his eyes.

Gregor turned off the light and left the farmhouse, climbing into the back of his van, scrambling into a heavy sleeping bag. He wished he could sleep in the house, but dare not, close to his aunt; his guilt too great.

"They will pay for my having to quieten aunt Julie." He wouldn't allow himself to sleep upstairs. His final exit from the farmhouse, after the trial, allowed little time for escape, and he couldn't guarantee to destroy every shred of DNA evidence upstairs after punishing the guilty.

In the morning, without re-entering the house, Gregor drove through to York and waited a short distance away from Stamford's house. Just after midday he came out of the house and walked past Gregor. He decided to leave the car and follow Stamford on foot. When he turned the corner Stamford was stood at a bus stop with two other people behind him In the queue as the bus drew up which Gregor had to run for.

Stamford had gone upstairs with Gregor sat downstairs halfway along the bus in a rear facing seat able to see everyone that came down. The bus entered the town centre and at the third stop Stamford alighted with Gregor following on at a reasonable distance.

Eventually Stamford entered the local job centre while Gregor waited across the road in a doorway. He came out of the centre and caught a bus back home. Gregor moved his car to another part of the street where no one overlooked him, still with a good view of Stamford's house.

At six thirty without further movement from inside, Gregor decided to call it a day and drove back to his aunt's farmhouse.

He turned on the light, their blindfolds helping them adjust to the brilliance, and he took the bowls from beneath their chairs; emptied them and returned them. After removing Railton's hat, he placed a head set over the Judges ears with music playing, loud enough so that he couldn't hear the conversation he was about to have with Railton. "You must be hungry now the beers worn off. I can see now, after following you for several days why you need to generate exorbitant fees. You spend it all on booze. You're an alcoholic. A criminals best friend, but because of it you are now on trial. I will remove your tape so that you can eat but fire any questions at me and you get nothing to eat until tomorrow."

It immediately started. "What the hell's happening?" Why am I here?"

Crack!! --As Railton groggily shook his head, Gregor held his Fist in pain. "Bastard." then quickly replaced the tape across his mouth. "I can't be bothered threatening you with chloroform. You don't eat now until tomorrow night."

His blindfold was replaced and headphones attached but not until Gregor had to punch him in the mouth again to still him. Railton, with his large frame tried angrily with all his might to rock the chair back and forth. It never moved.

Gregor removed the Judges hat and tape and fed and watered him without question as he watched the new prisoner attempting to lurch from side to side, mumbling unintelligibly from behind his gag.

"You're learning" he said as he replaced the tape and hat. He turned out the light and went to sleep in the van.

The following day Stamford never came out of his house until six pm., just as Gregor was about to give up on him. Following him on foot along several streets he entered a convenience store and came out carrying a plastic carrier bag. Gregor observed him as he walked around the back of the shop into a dimly lit alleyway. Remaining unnoticed, Gregor stood behind a bush and waited as Stamford took a bottle of cider from the carrier and slipped the bag into his pocket. He unscrewed the top and took a long drink, as though his life depended upon it. Gregor thought that this could present an opportunity to join him and considered going into the shop to purchase a bottle of cider but decided against it with the shops CCTV cameras, even though he was still disguised. He hurried along to another shop a half mile away to buy one, hoping that Stamford would still be in the alley when he returned.

Walking back in he apologised to Stamford asking if he didn't mind sharing the alley as he was in desperate need of a drink.

"Only if you give me a swig."

Gregor noticed only a couple of mouthfuls of cider remained in Stamfords bottle. "Be my guest" he said passing his bottle across. He took a long drink and gave it back.

"Haven't seen you around here before." said Stamford.

"I'm just staying at a friends for a few nights. Had to move out of my flat at the other side of town; too much shit happening. But God was I ready for this." said Gregor as he passed it back. Stamford had another long swig, put the bottle down and walked across to a bush saying he needed a piss.

Gregor couldn't believe his luck and quickly pulled a miniature bottle out of his pocket that contained the date rape drug; G.H.B., pouring it into the cider and pretending to drink it as Stamford returned.

"Give me another drink. I really am gagging today."

Gregor let him hold onto the bottle until after five minutes he fell against the wall and slowly slithered down it, not allowing the bottle to slip from his grasp even as his ability to function physically abandoned him. Gregor shook him without response and after taking the bottle from him, pulled him behind the bush and left him sat up with the cider bottle at his side so it wouldn't look suspicious if someone came across him while Gregor went for his car. He quickly returned, driving down the alley and two minutes later was driving away again, having expected to follow Stamford for another two or three days while thinking of a way to ensnare him.

Safely shackled to a third chair, gagged and blindfolded, Gregor emptied the bowls from beneath Bower and Railton's chairs into the large empty open topped drum that stood in the corner, before removing Railton's hat to be greeted by a decidedly icy stare.

"That's better. You're not so sure of yourself now are you? I'm the one calling the shots. Yes, you want to know why you're here, and in time I'll tell you but until that point you don't give me any grief like you did yesterday or you're for it, and I'm not going to hurt my fist like I did yesterday, I'll hit you with a fucking hammer next time, and don't think I won't. I'm going to take the tape off your mouth and although you'll want to ask me a lot of questions don't say a word."

Gregor affixed the head phones once again over the Judges ears and also to Stamford's ears in case he came to, before he turned back to Railton. "The tape's coming off so that you can eat." Gregor walked across the room and returned with a hammer that he placed in front of Railton. He went to the fridge to get his sandwich as Railton stared at the other two. Gregor removed the tape and fed his prisoner from the tongs as Railton stared at the hammer.

After drinking his water Gregor re-taped his mouth without a word before replacing the blindfold and attaching headphones.

He attended to the Judge who fearfully eyed Gregor while eating in silence. Once he had eaten, Gregor turned out the light and left them alone with their thoughts.

The following morning Gregor entered the cellar and one by one removed the three blindfolds, watching their reactions. Both the Judge and solicitor eyed each other in bewildering curiosity; then simultaneously switched their gaze to Stamford, unaware of who he was but appeared vaguely familiar. Gregor remained quiet until he held all their stares and then took his own seat.

"I see you two recognise each other. You Mr. Stamford can see the corrupt solicitor who so expensively attempted to defend you. Your father wasted his money. He tried to fool the jury into returning a not guilty verdict and, I've noted several of his cases where he has been much more devious. I'm sure you'll also recognise the Judge who handed down your sentence. As for you Judge Bowers and solicitor Railton, you perhaps might be wondering why you are both present here. By the look on your faces it is obvious that you've seen Stamford before, but unsure of where from. Yes, I can see the lines of hard thought spread across both your foreheads, desperately to remember him. It might not be so easy judge Bowers as he was before you ten years ago, but I relive it all the time. I can still picture the look of none caring on Stamford's face when he murdered my cousin whilst riding his bike."

Gregor momentarily held his nose. "My God the stench in here is overwhelming. Still you won't have to suffer it for much longer." He moved across to Judge Bowers and removed his gag who only stared back in silence. He took Railton's tape from his mouth who immediately started firing questions. "What do you intend to do with us? We've done nothing wrong."

"That will be decided by the court."

"Which court?"

"The court that you sit before now."

"We've no case to answer. For God's sake let us go."

"You will all be given a fair trial. Now be quiet or you'll feel my hammer. Ten years ago, while cycling, my cousin James Durakovic was knocked from his cycle and died from his injuries. Donald Stamford, who held neither a driving licence nor insurance, and, while under the influence of alcohol killed James and unbelievably pleaded not guilty."

Gregor looked at Railton. "By your direction, forcing his mother to sit through the trial. You assured his father that you would convince the jury to find him innocent and stretched the hours out and your fee up."

"I remember the case and------"

"Shut up!!" Gregor screamed "If you say another word I'll hammer you. And you Judge Bowers, what prison term would you impose if your son had been killed by someone driving in an irresponsible way, who never held a driving licence and was under the influence of alcohol?"------"Your hesitation says it all. James' mother was destroyed twice. Once by Stamford, and secondly by you, by the inadequate sentence that you passed on him. What have you to say?"

"I remember the case but sometimes our

hands are tied by legislation; minimum and maximum sentences and any other contributory factors. I seem to recall James had a greater amount of alcohol in his system and unable to know for certain if he'd swayed outwards led to me not passing a longer sentence."

"Your hands are tied now and justice will be served."

"What do you intend to do with us all?" the Judge asked. "What purpose would harming us serve if James' mother was traumatised once, then to go through all that trauma again for your actions towards us would serve no use at all."

The judge screamed in pain as his knee cap cracked under the hammer, Gregor's face flaring in anger.

"Don't you dare try and put that on me you scheming bastard, pretending that she'll feel the guilt when in reality you attempt to aim that very same feeling towards me." he screamed even louder. "His mother's body is rotting in the next room. Apart from my guilt from silencing her I have no other guilt. As I promised, you will each have a fair trial, but I assure you leniency is lost on me, so state your case carefully. You

Judge Bowers, have just lost your case and I find you guilty of incompetence and you will serve no further part in the proceedings."

Gregor replaced the tape across his mouth to silence his groaning. "I will sentence you later."

"Railton, how are you able to sleep at night. Do you ever think on the pain you impose on the families of those who suffer. Your corrupt interpretation of the law allows many criminals to walk free from the court with a smile upon their faces. I remember Stamford's face, the smile he could hardly hide as his sentence was passed. I hold you personally responsible. You had the audacity to advise him to plead not guilty, attempting to switch the blame onto my cousin as he had had a drink. You have a way of getting your deceit across to the jury without spotting your trickery. Convince me now of your innocence; your life depends on it."

"Regardless of any words I may find, I feel my fate has already been decided. I have a responsibility to any client that I represent to defend them to the best of my ability, and if I know of their guilt I try to minimise their sentence with my representation, to one that truly reflects the level of their crime but I am still legally bound to act on their behalf. I still act with more impartiality than that which you bring to your own court today. You are emotionally and personally connected to the case and that would never be allowed in a British court of law where a Judge, solicitor or juror was involved. That is one of the reasons why the British legal system is so respected worldwide. In any case before a court, people connected to the case will all have different views on the outcome, whether won or lost, and as much as I am sorry that the case of your cousin has led to this day, I represented my client in a fair and legal manner, with him never-the-less being found guilty."

Gregor, with his hand wrapped around his chin as he thought, looked directly at Railton without speaking. Eventually he turned towards Stamford before he rose and walked across to Railton who stared, attempting not to show his fear. Gregor replaced the tape over his mouth. "I will not be accused of impartiality." He walked over to Stamford and removed his tape. Gregor stared threateningly into his eyes.

"You have heard the case, and each one will

be dealt with fairly. I know after your trial, even for the short sentence that you had imposed, in some people's eyes, they felt you were wrongly convicted. You have the chance shortly to state your case, but you now act as Judge. Do you find Railton innocent or guilty?"

Stamford looked in fear at the solicitor, then across to Judge Bowers, who behind his tape, grimaced with pain. Close to tears he whispered "I find him guilty" he said almost apologetically.

"I agree with you and will hand sentence down later. And now for your case Mr.Stamford. Do you think that your sentence sufficed your crime?"

"I know that you---". His excuses were immediately cut off by tape roughly strewn across his mouth by Gregor. "Do you think that I'm going to give you the opportunity to speak when your guilt is already established? I witnessed it you idiot".

Gregor walked to the back of the cellar as all heads turned to follow him. He unscrewed the plastic cap from a petrol container and spread it around everyone's feet as each prisoner slammed their ankles against the chains in sheer panic, attempting wildly to free their wrists from the handcuffs whilst trying desperately to rock the chairs from their grounding, their efforts futile.

Gregor poured the second container around the backs of each chair, pouring a third across all of their laps as they shook their heads at him in a begging fashion, unable to speak although still attempting to shout through the tape in anguish. He climbed the stairs before tossing a lighted matchbox down to witness the immediate flare enflame panicking bodies before closing the heavy cellar door. Gregor quickly poured out three more containers of petrol around the ground floor of the house and looked in sorrow to his aunt as he threw another lighted matchbox onto the petrol before closing the door behind him. He emptied two more containers of fuel, one into the back of the van, the other into the drivers cab, set them alight and trotted without panic three hundred yards into the back lane where his car with its false number plates was parked. That night the farmhouse fire unfolded on the local television news.

Discovery of the bound and gagged bodies brought the world's media scrambling the following day, and a day later it was announced that through an inscription found on the watch of one victim, a unique ring worn by another and dental records of a third victim confirmed they were the three people kidnapped.

"Jesus, we thought the kidnappings around the country might possibly take the media pressure off us slightly regarding the Midlands murders; Instead the poor bastards wind up barbequed on our patch. Why Birmingham?" demanded Turner.

"Another team are being drafted in from the West Mercia Police; we haven't the manpower to give a hundred percent to both cases" said Chief Superintendent Burns. "We need a breakthrough in our investigation; the pressure's on now from upstairs after the killing of Lynn Tudor and subsequent arrest of John Stamp. As far as they were concerned, it was a job well done but with the following murders by Stamps' accomplice or accomplices, the feeling is we're not pushing Stamp enough to make him crack."

A letter arrived at The Daily Mirror's offices which read:

I STRUCK TO RIGHT ALL WRONGS COMMITED BY THOSE IN PLACE WHOSE JOB IT WAS TO PUNISH THE GUILTY OF THEIR CRIMES. THE INADEQUATE SENTENCE PASSED DOWN DESTROYED BOTH VICTIM AND FAMILY ALIKE. THEIR INCOMPETENCE WAS THEIR OWN UNDOING.

-----------SATAN----------

CHAPTER TWENTY-FIVE

Arnold was sat at home, frustrated, awaiting the date when he would be required to attend the inquiry into his conduct. He was kept informed of how the case was going by one of his colleagues, Scott. But apart from a renewed appeal for anyone to contact the police regarding a red Fiat Punto with tinted rear windows there was nothing else to tell.

Arnold had an idea, and started scouring burial records.

Jack walked through the cemetery to where Karina was buried knowing it would not be long before he was back with her; the day he longed for as revenge for her was near completion. Hardy had been located in Brighton, working in a local bakery. Jack carried his usual twelve roses, the only flower in life that she loved. He had managed to visit her several days earlier and knew the flowers he had lain down then would still be reasonably fresh but, not knowing how long he would be away taking care of Hardy in Brighton, decided to renew them. He passed through the cemetery, walking between headstones old and new, some small and others nearing five feet. As he walked past two of the larger ones he could see where Karina was laid to rest. Jack stopped dead in his tracks quickly ducking back behind the tall gravestones as someone was at Karina's grave, half knelt down feeling the roses. His back was turned towards Jack, who kept quiet.

"I wonder what you would have made of it all?, people murdered to avenge your lifestyle. I wonder if you would have approved? I doubt it. The roses have not been here long which proves to me that Jack, whoever he is still visits you regularly. For all the care he has taken to avoid leaving any clues, the fool actually comes to your graveside. I know from what I've been told it could be no-one else as you had no relatives living locally, and few friends. This is where we will catch your psychopathic avenger."

As he rose, Jack recognised him instantly and as he retreated, under his breath muttered " how the hell did you discover who Karina was? Stamp could never have guessed who it was about. The police are closer than I thought and Hardy has to be dealt with first. I must not be caught."

He arrived home cursing and slammed the door in anger. "I wanted so much to visit her resting place when all the parasites had been dealt with, to talk with her before I went to her and now that's been taken away. Arnold will pay."

Jack broke down crying then screamed out as if in agony, his emotions in turmoil. "I'll kill the bastard!!"He head butted the wall and a cut opened up on his forehead. He butted it again and again until the blood streamed down his face into his eyes.

CHAPTER TWENTY-SIX

Tom Hardy's movements had been monitored for several days and Ricky was sat in the van at five a.m. waiting for him to take his usual route, walking along the small quiet street on his way to work. As he came into view through the vans rear mirror, Ricky got out and opened the back doors coinciding with Hardy passing by. He never knew what hit him. Ricky threw the pipe Into the van next to the motorbike before he dragged Hardy's unconscious body in alongside. As he drove away he cursed himself for having got rid of the tazer gun, needing to use the pipe, unsure if he'd already killed him, requiring him to be alive so that he could be confronted with his sins. Hardy would then be forced to beg for forgiveness from God enabling Jack to save his soul.

He came to, groaning, and attempted to raise his right hand to his aching head instantly realising they were held together behind his back, bound with plastic tie wraps, his ankles held in the same way.

"Where am I? What's happening?"

"You'll find out shortly; we're nearly there."

"What's happening? Where are we going?"

"You've asked that question once!!" Ricky screamed.

"Say another word and I'll hit you with the pipe again."

A few minutes later the van turned onto a large, long disused airfield, desolate, way into the countryside. At Its centre Ricky turned off the ignition, walked around to the back and pulled Hardy out who landed in a crumpled heap at his feet. Hardy looked at him, terror running through his veins, not daring to say anything as he was dragged from the ground to his feet.

"You destroyed my friend's life when you killed his wife driving like a maniac whilst drunk. What have you to say for yourself?"

"I'm so sorry. I didn't mean to harm anyone. I spent three years inside and she was all I thought about every day."

"You thought about her only because she was the reason you were behind bars. You blamed her; you felt no remorse, and now you're sorry because you're frightened of what I'll do to you."

"I really am sorry."

"Her husband is a forgiving type of guy, and as hard as it was and still is he wants you to ask God for forgiveness for your sins."

Hardy looked on unsure of what to do.

Ricky shrieked " Well, I'm waiting!!"

"Please God forgive me."

"For what?"

"For accidentally killing that woman."

Ricky climbed back into the van, started the engine and wound his window down." There's two plastic tie wraps between your ankles so you can take six inch steps. You're free to go but you'll have to walk." He wound the window back up again and drove off.

Hardy was so relieved to see the van drive out of sight and started the long walk to the airfield's perimeter. Half an hour later when he was close to its edge the van reappeared and stopped next to him.

"I got it wrong. Apparently you have to feel what it was like for Karina, so I'll rev it up to seventy miles an hour and if you reach the edge of the airfield first you're safe."

"Please don't. I'll never make it."

"Strange; Karina didn't either."

The van screeched off towards the runway and made a U turn, gathering speed rapidly as Hardy desperately shuffled his feet. The van hit him from behind at great speed which threw him up in the air landing fifteen feet away, one foot appearing to be twisted right around, and his left trouser leg split open by a protruding bone. When the van drew up alongside him, Hardy was groaning.

"God you're a toughie. Karina died at the first hit."

The van was driven around again, and at twenty miles an hour ran over him twice before being parked up next to Hardy's lifeless body. Ricky rolled the motorbike from out the back of the van before putting Hardy inside, and after pouring petrol both inside and outside the van, set it alight. The flames and smoke were visible for miles as the bike roared off.

The following day Jack was deep in thought and as usual, spoke out softly to himself.

"I wish I had met Karina a lot earlier, before she had been led down the path into temptation; so much innocence corrupted. If she had really been my wife she would have wanted for nothing."

"She wasn't your wife!!?" Ricky screamed.

Jack hadn't realised he was in the room and he held his breath in fear, not daring to turn around to face Ricky.

"Answer me. Please tell me you're lying."

"Ricky, I'm so sorry. I loved Karina as if she was my wife. I know I've lied to you but I felt as if she really was mine. She could never be. We never even made love. She said I was the only man she trusted; the only man that she shared her innermost secrets with, but to have had sex I would become no better than the rest of her clients in her eyes. I longed for her and imagined such a beautiful life together. I didn't mean to lie to you."

"You didn't mean to lie to me? You've let me kill six fucking people because you let me believe they'd destroyed your wife. That's the strength of my loyalty as a friend towards you, and it was all lies; all fucking lies! You hadn't even slept together."

"I'd never intended to deceive you. Karina wasn't even her real name but it was the one she preferred; the one her clients called her by."

"I don't believe what I'm hearing. You mug; you were no more than one of her punters. She thought so little of you she wouldn't even allow you to use her real name. What was it?"

"Sharon."

"Sharon Fall?" asked Ricky.

"It was for a while but how did you know that?"

"The watch you always clasp so tightly; her name's engraved on it. I've always wondered about it but never asked."

"She only held that surname for a little over two years until she divorced him."

"Divorced who?"

"An African called Dede Fall. Sharon was persuaded into a marriage of convenience so he could get British nationality. She didn't know him but received a thousand pounds to do it. When she divorced him, she reverted to her maiden name; Sharon Peterson. She was also briefly married at eighteen, her name then being Smith."

"Jesus! It gets worse by the minute. It's all in your twisted little mind. I bet in some warped thought somewhere in that stupid brain of yours you actually think you are married. I bet she's up there now looking down on us, laughing so much it hurts. I can't believe what you've allowed me to do for you. She was never yours. Can't you see she's used you? You've told me over and over that you gave her all your money, and you never even got to shag her; her a prostitute and all you got was a kiss."

"It doesn't hurt anyone my being alone with my thoughts. That's the only way I can have her."

"Try telling that to the families of six dead people that it doesn't hurt anyone."

"Karina has been fully avenged. They've all paid their earthly price; It's in God's hands now.

Ricky don't leave me. I need you more than you could know".

Jack hurried out of the room into the lounge where he took Karina's watch from a drawer and held it close to his chest. "Darling I so want to be with you and it won't be long until we are back together." He raised it to his lips and kissed it tenderly. He went back through.

"Your planning's getting sloppy as well. Hardy's murder wasn't clearly thought through like the others were. Even though the van was burnt inside and out, what if the police are able to trace it back to you?"

"Ricky it doesn't matter" he said crying, "before the police realise it was me I'll have taken my own life to be back with Karina."

"Is this a wind-up? What am I supposed to do? You can't kill yourself."

"That's the way I had always planned it."

"There's no wonder you wanted me to kill them all. I thought it was just your weird righteous morals. Oh no! It was more than that. You didn't want to offend your God in case he denied you entry into his world. You've used me and now you're going to dump me. I won't allow it!"

"You can't stop me." Jack walked across to the bathroom cabinet and took out a box of pills. He sat down with a glass of water picturing Karina in his mind, the only thing he wanted to concentrate on.

"Don't you dare take them!" Ricky screamed. "You are not going to desert me now!"

"Ricky you've helped me through some really low points in my life and done things for me that I had no right to ask of you but I have to go my own way now."

Jack tried to take the tablets but kept them firmly in his hand, unable to do it.

"To go to her; that evil cow. Look at the sinful life she's led; a liar, a drug addict and a prostitute. Do you really think she'll be waiting in the world you're destined for? Ha!! She'll be shagging the Devil As we speak."

"Then I will see her again. Yes you murdered all the parasites, but they were all my planning and I will go to the same Hell where she is waiting for me. I must be back with Karina."

He raised his hand again to take the tablets, but try as he did, couldn't put them into his mouth. He threw them at the wall, angry with himself or Ricky, he wasn't sure and fell to the floor sobbing, apologising to God and Karina, angry with himself at his inability to take his own life, where against God's will, had allowed so many other lives to be taken.

CHAPTER TWENTY-SEVEN

Several days later Arnold received a phone call from Scott. "You're not going to believe this. We were contacted today from the Sussex police. They've questioned Mike Robinson over the murder of a guy called Tom Hardy. He'd been murdered and then his body set alight. He was identified from his dental records after being reported missing."

"Have they charged him?"

"Afraid not. He was only questioned in the first place because four years ago Hardy accidentally killed Robinson's girlfriend in a car accident and had been threatened by Robinson in court. Hardy got out of prison six months ago. Robinson never mentioned the fact that he had been helping us with our enquiries and the only way that they found out was when his DNA was tested and placed on the data base. Dave it was the same result so the sample that he gave to us couldn't have been mixed up at the laboratory."

"Damn! ------- what was his girlfriends name?", asked Arnold.

"Sharon Fall."

"Jesus, I thought we had him then. Have you had any joy from the graveyard stakeout?"

" Nothing at all."

Heavily disguised, Jack waited in the cold damp weather day after day, sat out of view on the public garden bench that overlooked the main entrance to the Coventry Central police station. He knew Arnold had been suspended from duty as it had appeared on the news, but unable to find him in the telephone directory, felt this would be his best chance of locating him. He sat there wondering how they could have fathomed out Karina's connection. A thought came to him. "Electoral register!" then equally as fast realised neither he nor Karina were registered. Then it hit him; "Arnold will be!"

The frost lay over most of the cars parked along SilverAvenue, their windscreens iced over. Jack's screen was clear and had been since seven a.m. He had driven the short distance into Arnold's street and parked in one of several places available, between the cars, fifty yards before the Arnold's house, and unable to be spotted, he could easily see his home. At nine thirty, the D.C.I. And his wife came out, climbed into their car and drove off. Jack stayed.

After ten minutes, still heavily disguised, having checked there were no security cameras outside Arnold's or any of the neighbouring houses, he knocked loudly upon the front door. No answer, he knocked several times again, until the adjoining front door opened.

"I think they are both out." exclaimed their neighbour.

"What a shame; I'm only visiting the area and thought I'd drop in on Harry."

"I think you must have the wrong address. Dave and Fiona Arnold live here."

"Don't they have a son called Harry?"

"No. They only have one lad. His name is Simon and he lives in York. Dave and Fiona live by themselves."

Jack apologised saying he'd been given the address by another friend which was obviously wrong.

He came away having learnt exactly what he was after.

Dave and Fiona had been waiting twenty minutes to see the specialist regarding the results of the further DNA test. Fiona had been going out of her mind with worry and hadn't said a word to Simon.

They were beckoned into the specialist's office.

"Mr. and Mrs. Arnold, firstly I must apologise for the trauma you both must have been going through. I'm pleased to tell you that the problem has been resolved. Your saliva sample that we sent for analysis has come back showing you do carry the same DNA trace as Simon so it is beyond doubt that you are his biological mother."

"So it is possible for samples to get mixed up." said Dave angrily.

"No, that's not the case. What has come to light is a rarity, and I have never seen anything like it. Fiona you have what is called Chimera. You carry two different counts of DNA."

"How is that possible?" she asked.

"Research shows that at the point of Simon's conception you would have released two eggs generating twins but before the embryo's could form, both eggs would have fused into one, so becoming one child, but carrying two different counts of DNA., the second count, you could say, coming from the sibling, as in the fused egg. A reversal if you like of identical twins, who come from the same egg that splits into two. When the first sample was taken from your blood for screening, your other DNA count remained hidden. When the second sample, that of saliva was taken and analysed, your second count emerged with the first DNA count remaining hidden."

As they came away from the specialist's office Arnold held his wife tightly, the relief apparent on her face.

"That's such good news. God knows what was going through your mind, but I'm so pleased that you found out before you go to Simons this afternoon for a few days on a surprise visit."

As they came away from the hospital Dave explained that Tom Hopewell had rung and sounded down.

"I want to make sure he's okay and said I'd meet him in the Crown pub for a few games of pool if that's okay with you. Obviously I first needed to make certain everything was alright at the hospital and I'm so relieved."

"Me too. I'm so pleased it's all worked out fine and it's alright. Take us home, jump on a bus to the Crown and I'II get a taxi to take me to the station later."

Jack remained parked down Silver Street, just past Arnold's house. He wiped his tears away before clenching his fists. "I'll show you. I can't kill myself and am no longer able to visit Karina. My world is at an end, but I will rejoin her. After you discover your wife has been murdered you will do the deed for me that I cannot bring myself to do."

Dave Arnold came out and walked across to a bus stop. When the bus arrived Arnold got on with Jack in slow pursuit. Two miles away down a busy approach road to the town centre he left the bus and entered the Crown pub. Jack parked his car and walked past, looking in and seeing Arnold and a friend setting up the pool table. He drove back to their house and knocked heavily at the door. Fiona answered it, an anxious look on her face.

" Mrs. Arnold, Dave's been hurt in an accident outside the Crown pub. An ambulance has taken him to the hospital. The landlord asked me to rush round to take you to his side."

"Oh my God. How badly is he hurt?" she asked, hurriedly climbing into the car.

"I'm not sure but the ambulance was on the scene quickly. His friend went with him in the ambulance."

Sat in the back she pulled out her mobile to ring Simon. Jack reached behind and snatched it from her, immediately snapping the central locking on.

"What's happening?" she demanded. "What are you doing? Where's Dave?"

Jack drove on in silence after pressing the lock controlling the electric windows. "Who are you for God's sake?" He drove on without a word.

Fiona pulled and pulled at the door handle without success. She attempted to pull the lock up from the door. It remained in position. She reached across to the other rear door attempting the same; again it refused to move.

"Please let me out." she begged. Jack drove on.

Later that evening, Arnold was relaxing, enjoying his space. With Fiona at Simons he decided to go on line and typed in-- Chimera / Dual DNA. The answers were immediate, and after five minutes sifting through the information, a line came up confirming his suspicions. "Anyone with different coloured eyes has a high probability of being a chimera. I knew it!" he exclaimed with an air of victory. *His second sample by the Sussex force would have made no difference; the same sample of saliva and hair would have been taken producing the same results. We need Blood or a different bodily sample.*

Arnold immediately rang his super to explain his findings but before he had hardly started talking, Chief Superintendent Burns interrupted him. "Dave I appreciate your efforts and concern but you're off the case now and we're trying to contain the damage already done through Robinson's solicitor-----"

"But Robinson's guilty. You're not listening. Another type of DNA sample will prove he's the murderer."

"Dave we can't be certain of that and you more than anyone will realise that we would be refused one by the suspect or the court. There's another appeal in the media tomorrow for a Fiat Punto with tinted windows-------"

"Robinson's guilty, can't you see?" said Arnold breaking in.

"D.C.I. Arnold you've not only been taken off the case because of your very damaging illegal attempt to pursue one member of the general public but also because there's a feeling within your own team that your views are blinkered and unchangeable, bordering on paranoia."

Arnold slammed the phone down. "All the damn years I've given them. All the criminals I've brought to justice and the only thanks I get is a knife in the back."

He thought about his colleague, sergeant Tom Hopewell and pictured his daughter in happier times. The image in his mind switched to her as she had been found in the woods, her throat deeply cut and his anger came to a head. He was not drunk but well on the way and without thinking climbed into his car. "The bastard will not get away with it; I'll confront him and wipe that arrogant smile off his face."

Knocking on Robinson's door, he opened it, and seeing Arnold attempted to close it just as fast but not before Arnold wedged his foot in. He grabbed Robinson by the throat thrusting him backwards against the hallway wall. "You think you've got away with it don't you?"

Robinson pulled Arnold's hand away from him allowing him to cough and splutter as the air rushed out.

"Get out of my house, you're drunk. My solicitor will make certain you lose your job for this. Its continual harassment. Where will you be then with no-one to bully?"

The anger rose too high and with a right hook he split Robinson's nose with an almighty crack as the blood spurted upwards into the air. Arnold stormed out leaving Robinson sat groaning on the floor.

Back at home, the seriousness of his actions came to him. He had never allowed himself to get too close to any case in the past as he realised the significance of Robinson's words, knowing that it would cost him his job. He put his head in his hands and looked to the floor; then he saw it. Robinson's blood had landed on the bottom of his trouser leg. He thought for a while but realising he had nothing to lose, rang Scott at the station. "Has the shit hit the fan yet?"

"I don't know what you mean Dave."

"I expect a complaint to come through soon from Robinson's solicitor. I've decked him so I think I'll be out on my ear."

"Dave I don't know what to say."

"The thing is Robinson has two DNA counts. We initially thought there was a mix up of the samples and sent Robinson's specimen's off again as you know, which after analysis came back showing the same result. What we needed to do was send a different bodily sample instead of the usual mouth swab or hair and I can prove it."

"Dave you're losing me. I don't get it."

"Robinson has a genetic condition called Chimera, which means a dual DNA count. I can't go into it all right now but it's been proven as he has different coloured eyes. When we've finished talking get it up on line. Scott we can actually prove Robinson's the murderer and that he acted along with Stamp. When I hit him his blood spilled onto my trousers which needs analysing but we aren't allowed any further DNA tests against Robinson as the courts wont issue a warrant. If we don't prove his guilt he will go on killing so we've got to get his blood analysed. Scott I can't expect you to send it off but I've nothing to lose if you send it off in my name. You'll have to get your hands on the results as soon as they are returned if you're willing to do it."

"Of course I am. Apart from bringing Robinson to justice it could be the only way of saving your Job. I'll come straight round for it."

CHAPTER TWENTY-EIGHT

Robinson's solicitor put In a strong complaint and Arnold was arrested, questioned, and later released, while Chief Superintendent Burns kept well out of the way, angry at Arnold's stupidity.

Arnold was sat thinking. *I daren't ring Fiona at Simons to tell her what's happened; it'll spoil her stay and she'll come straight back home; better we talk face to face when she gets back.*

The results came through with a positive match from Robinson's DNA to the blood left at the murder scene of Farrell. Scott took them straight round to Arnold's, and Arnold drove to the station and marched into the Chief Superintendent's office.

"Dave what are you doing here?"

"Sir I have the proof here that Robinson is the murderer. It's just been returned from the laboratory."Burns looked at him a little cautiously. "Dave you're off the case. What's it all about?"

Arnold placed the DNA results before him.

The superintendent shook his head. "You were right all along, they can get mixed up but why has it taken so long to come to light?" he asked as he raised his head to look at Arnold.

"Sir, I tried explaining that Robinson has a duel DNA count and another type of sample was required for analysis. These results came from his blood, not his saliva or hair."

The Superintendent looked over his glasses at Arnold." I was thinking this lab result was perhaps an oversight on their behalf, please tell me it was."

"The sample came from my clothes after I hit him."

"I don't believe what I'm hearing; entrapment again, and this time while you're suspended, having been arrested for assaulting him in the first place to obtain your sample. Have you lost all senses?"

"I knew it was him. What did you want me to do? Nothing; let him go on killing?

"I'll have to consult our legal team immediately although I'm already convinced the DNA result would be inadmissible in court----"

"The man's killed six people---"

"And it will be your idiotic fault if he can't be brought to justice."

Arnold stormed out.

Chief Superintendent Burns met with the Midlands Police Authority lawyers, bringing them up to date and after considering their legal options the decision was unanimous. " With all the bad publicity surrounding the Midland's murders plus, with the Independent police Complaints Commission which starts the investigation tomorrow into the handling of the case, especially the unlawful manner in which Robinson had been hounded for a further DNA sample which he legally didn't have to provide, another slip up would be unacceptable. With what you're telling us now, that Arnold actually attacked him to get a blood sample for further analysis, the cases regarding Sharon Peterson unfortunately leaves Robinson untouchable without further evidence against him, away from DNA evidence. What the hell was Arnold thinking. Has he cracked up. The DNA fiasco would have it thrown out of court before proceedings were barely started."

An hour later a call came through to the station from Dr. Hilton for acting D.C.I. Turner who took the call and asked how he could be of assistance.

"Inspector, after the conversation we had regarding Sharon Peterson, something of extreme importance has come to light where I find myself in an impossible situation concerning patient confidentiality but it is of the utmost urgency that you visit my office immediately."

Turner and Morgan were in his office twenty minutes later. "Doctor thanks for seeing us. What is it that you've discovered?"

"It wasn't initially regarding the murders centre'd around Sharon, but the disappearance and eventual murders of those tragically discovered at the farmhouse in Birmingham. I had to question my confidentiality commitment with my suspicions and initially decided not to approach you regarding a certain individual in case I was terribly wrong. Around ten years ago I treated a patient who had a problem with sentences handed down too leniently in his view for those who were responsible for unintentionally killing people. His hatred towards the judiciary was unbalanced, and, unchanged, could have resulted in his being sectioned, but fortunately after a course of therapy he had a complete turnaround in his views, enough to satisfy me that he posed no threat to others.

In his early teens he was heavily reliant upon cannabis which resulted in psychosis. In his late teens he developed schizophrenia which most probably evolved from the psychosis. He also developed dissociative identity disorder. A voice came into his mind, although not from a directing point as can sometimes occur; the voice in his head was more as a friend who he conversed with regularly. Some schizophrenics can be withdrawn and find communicating difficult leading to low self-esteem, not allowing them to develop many personal relationships. I believe his imaginary friend was initially a comfort to him, a substitute for friends he couldn't make until it became such a force within him that he actually believed in his existence. It would have been an alter ego. He called him Ricky. His dissociative identity disorder could have been a direct result of the continual physical abuse he suffered as a young child. While I was treating him one day he had another alter ego that went by the name of Gregor Natas and he even spoke with an Eastern European dialect. When he was better I asked who Gregor Natas was but he shook his head, completely unaware of him, excepting to say he must be an all powerful force, which is usually attributed to those suffering from schizophrenia. He said by the sound of the name he could be related to his aunts former husband who was a Bosnian.

He would say no more on the matter.

I have only just returned from holiday which is the reason why I have only now come forward not being aware of the circumstances of the murders. I wasn't convinced about sharing this information, because, as I said it was only a suspicion, but after discussing it with my wife who is also my secretary, she remembered something extremely important. She told me that she felt convinced that it was he who used to meet Sharon Peterson after her counselling sessions years after treating him. With his previous thoughts and feelings on judges and solicitors and his association with Sharon I had no hesitation in ringing you. I have no idea how this will be seen by the board but my moral obligations on this matter are far more important. His name is Michael Jack Robinson."

"Mike Robinson; and you say his middle name's Jack?"

"Yes, he preferred to be called Jack. Apparently his parents decided to call him by his middle name not long after his birth was registered and he stuck with it ever since."

"Do you think you would be able to recognise him in an identity parade?"

"I'm not really sure. I could try but if he's shaven his overgrown beard and moustache off it may be difficult."

"Did he have the beard and moustache when he used to meet Sharon Peterson after her counselling sessions."

"Yes he did. It used to cover half of his face."

" Do you think your wife might be able to

identify him without the beard?"

"I'll ask her but it's extremely doubtful. She only saw him a few times, and again with the beard."

"Would you have his address for that period?"

"I've already checked on that and it appears he was living rough with no fixed abode, apparently squatting."

"Doctor a note was received from the murderer of those burnt to death in the farmhouse, signed by Satan. Does that in any way connect with your patient?"

After brief consideration the doctor responded. "Yes it does. All those years ago when I was treating him, he told me how someone was regularly painting messages on his wall; always the same message. I remember what he told me as clear as day because of the bizarre wording.

Above the window it read;

INDIGNATION. JUDGEMENT AWAITS.

Below the window it read;

THE OMNIPOTENT.

Across the window it was signed;

SATAN.

He would have painted the words on himself in an oblivious state."

Turner thanked the doctor, ended the meeting and went to Chief Superintendent Burns office to explain the position.

"I don't believe it. Arnold's been in custody for attacking Robinson. We now know he's the murderer and I don't know if we can touch him. I'll get straight back on to the legal team; Arnold; stupid idiot.

Burns again met with the lawyers. After repeating their comments from their earlier meeting they added that In the case of the three murdered at the farmhouse; "yes, in ordinary circumstances bring any suspect in for questioning and for a new DNA sample,but once again in the absence of any proof and with the inquiry starting tomorrow around the events concerning Robinson, we feel that although the doctor says he met Sharon Peterson on several occasions the only connection to the farmhouse case is that of the note being signed by Satan; the same name of which the doctor says was written on Robinson's window years ago by someone other than himself, according to Robinson. Without the doctor or his wife possibly unable to pick Robinson out from an identity parade, it would be inadvisable to make him attend one. In our opinion it is not enough to bring him in for questioning without further evidence as it would only be viewed as continual harassment, fuelling additional ammunition for the inquiry. Search CCTV footage from every petrol station and motorway from the outskirts of Birmingham to every area from where each victim was taken, but if it fails to turn up a single sighting of Robinson's car then we'll be unable to arrest him ."

Burns came away from the meeting angry and frustrated, not at the unanimous decision to allow Robinson to remain free, more directed towards Arnold who had made a complete mess of the investigation. Scott rang Arnold to make him aware of the farmhouse murders connection.

He thanked Scott; ended the call and sat down in deep thought trying to make sense of it all.

Arnold was running the case through his mind when a text came through from Fiona's mobile.

OUR ROSE PETALS WERE SACROSANCT, BETWEEN ONLY HER AND ME.

THEY'RE NOW VIOLATED BY YOUR HANDS, INTRUDING OUR INFINITY.

FOR US TO TALK IN SECLUSION WAS ALL THAT I CRAVED,

BUT NOW I'M DEPRIVED OF THAT BY YOUR DESECRATION OF HER GRAVE.

MY HEART SCREAMS OUT IN ECHOES, SEPERATED TILL I DIE

TO BE REJOINED AS ONE WHEN I AM GONE, ON A PLANE SO HIGH.

YOUR PUNISHMENT FOR INTRUSION IS TO SUFFER THE SAME FATE

FOR THE MANY YEARS, AND COUNTLESS TEARS 'TIL YOU'RE AT HEAVANS GATE.

YOUR HEART WILL SCREAM IN ECHOES UNTIL THE ENDING OF YOUR LIFE

BECAUSE FOR YOU UNTIL THAT POINT, YOU WILL NEVER SEE YOUR WIFE.

He was momentarily stunned. "Jesus, the bastard's got Fiona!" He immediately rang her network to see if they could pinpoint its location.

Jack watched as the phone hit the canal and disappeared below the murky depths before driving back home.

Arnold screeched to a halt outside of Robinson's house and ran to the door barging through. Robinson froze having only arrived back himself moments earlier." Get out now. I'm ringing my solici----"

He fell to the floor banging his head, a heavy right hook from Arnold. "What have you done with my wife you bastard"? he screamed as he handcuffed him from behind.

" I haven't got a clue what you're talking about. Let me go."

"You don't know when to stop do you. Lie. Lie. Lie. That's all you can do. That and murder innocent People." Arnold spotted plastic tie wraps on the dining table and forced Robinson onto a chair. He then bound his wrists with the tie wraps through the chair's spell's before removing the handcuffs. He also tied his ankles to the chair. Arnold split his nose again with another right hook and in a continuous movement, brought his arm back up connecting his elbow with a sickening crunch onto Robinson's cheek bone.

"What have you done with my wife you bastard!!? Where is she?"

"I don't know where she is."

Crack! Arnold hit him hard to the mouth as Robinson spit out a front tooth. "You'd better not have harmed her."

"I've hurt no-one."

"You say that you're innocent. Without being able to find proof against you, the police continually hound you. Is that how you see it?"

He nodded, fearfully.

"But for all your pleading of innocence we both know you're the murderer. What you are not aware of is that evidence against you actually exists but because of a legal loophole is deemed inadmissible in court. You cannot be tried unless you kill again so allowing the DNA sampling process to re-start. My wife is not going to be the excuse for that to happen. Where is she!!?"

"I'm completely innocent. You can have no proof; I've never hurt anyone." Arnold kicked him in the groin. "Robinson you're guilty of the murder of six people around Sharon Peterson and the proof came from blood that landed on my trousers after punching you. It matches the blood from Farrell's office. You have two different counts of DNA but the court will not uphold the findings of the test. You're also responsible for the farmhouse killings. Where's my wife you lunatic?" Arnold cracked him hard across the head, and as Robinson winced, his head was swung viciously to a side by a heavy punch to his chin.

"I'll plead guilty; I'll give the police a statement."

Arnold studied Robinson's face. "You know the statement would be invalid, given under duress. Don't take me for an idiot."

"I'll give permission for another DNA sample to be taken."

"Only to change your mind again when I'm safely behind bars for kidnapping you."

Robinson's mouth moved to speak but a different voice uttered the words." He didn't kill them, I did."

Arnold, after being taken aback for a few seconds cracked Robinson once more.

"Leave him alone. He's done nothing wrong and he hasn't taken your wife; I did and I killed her."

Arnold screamed in anguish as he punched and kicked Robinson with such ferocity that the chair toppled over. Arnold grabbed it, pulling it upright, unaware of his own strength. "I'm going to fucking kill you and then I'm going to kill myself to be back with Fiona. You've destroyed my life you bastard!!"

"I want you to kill me. I deserve to die."

"No! He didn't kill them I did."

"Be quiet Ricky."

"No I'll plead guilty, don't kill him."

Arnold stepped back. "What sick game are you playing now?"

"Kill me. Avenge your wife as I have avenged Karina." pleaded Robinson.

Arnold stood there in confusion. "Karina?----
Who's Karina?" Arnold shook his head. "You're
asking me to kill you when you already know
that's my intention and then you pretend that
another person------"

"You can't kill him he didn't do anything; I
murdered them all."

"Ricky be quiet! I have to go to Karina now.
Please don't listen to Ricky, I have to die; I deserve
to die. I have tried to kill myself but cannot do
it. Please put me out of my misery; let me go to
Karina before you go to your wife."

"I really do believe that you want me to kill
you. Why did you murder so many people?"

"They destroyed my Karina."

"Lynn Tudor worked for a newspaper for
God's sake. and my wife never harmed a soul."

"I know. I'm so sorry. Please forgive me."

"You're one twisted bastard. You're a
paranoid schizophrenic." Arnold, shook his head
in disbelief and looked down into Robinson's
eyes. Robinson returned the stare, all traces of
his earlier fear gone, only dark and uncaring.

"I'll not kill you to give you the quick release to be back with the woman in whose name you butchered so many people. God knows how she ever endured you. Do you seriously think she'd want to spend the rest of eternity with a nutter like you? Believe me, she'll know how well off she is without you."

Robinson's eyes were ablaze with rage as he twisted and turned in a desperate attempt to be free of his bonds to kill once again.

Arnold heard another voice come from Robinson's lips with an Eastern European accent. "I am the all powerful Satan. Release me and I shall let you live." His voice returned to normal. "Please kill me; let me go to Karina."

"No I will not kill you. Instead I will give the police the evidence they need to lock you away for ever so that you can spend all day, every day with tortured thoughts and longings."

Arnold rang his colleague. "Scott, I'm at Robinson's. He's murdered Fiona." he said as tears streamed down his face." I was going to kill him, but I realise that's what the sick bastard wants so he can be back with his tart. Instead I'm going to die and make it look like he's murdered me so that you can legally take a fresh DNA sample with it being a new crime," every word spoken while looking directly into Robinson's eyes, ablaze with anger and frustration as he struggled to be free.

Scott interrupted loudly, shouting at the end of the line, panicking. "Dave, listen to me. Don't do anything foolish; we'll find a way to nail him."

"Listen to me Scott. Robinson's punishment is to live. I'll make certain the evidence to convict him is in place. Have the police car siren blasting out as they approach. That's the precise time that I die allowing Robinson neither time for escape or the chance to hide the evidence."

"Dave don't do it------"

"I've nothing to live for now. Hurry Scott." he said quietly as he hung up. He walked into the kitchen returning with a carving knife, held through a cloth to make certain of not leaving his finger prints on it. He walked behind Robinson who was swaying his head from side to side frantically, trying to see what Arnold was doing. He felt the knife slash across the back of his arm which released a small amount of blood that Arnold rubbed his shirt sleeve into, making certain that it also dripped onto the carpet.

Robinson's hopeless attempt of escape continued.

Doctor Hilton rang the station again and D.S. Turner took the call. "I've been thinking about Robinson with a feeling that somehow a clue was within the wording on his wall. It just came to me.

The words; INDIGNATION.JUDGEMENT AWAITS, suggest that whoever supposedly wrote it was a powerful enough figure to change the outcome of those wronged, possibly the OMNIPOTENT, overseer of everything; but never SATAN as he would certainly be powerful enough if he existed,----but a do-gooder;-- impossible. It would be the exact opposite of what the devil stood for. Robinson told me that he used to stare for hours at the words. He would have stared at the wording from inside his house, but the only word he would have seen was the name Satan, written across the window, the other words being outside on the brick. From inside the house he stared at the name Satan but the wording would have appeared back to front; NATAS; the exact opposite of SATAN. That is where he took the name from."

Turner immediately informed Burns who contacted the police lawyers, who in turn decided it was enough and gave the go-ahead for Robinson's arrest. Scott rang Arnold's number even though the police cars would arrive at Robinson's any second.

" Dave don't do it. We've got the missing link enabling us to nail Robinson."

" Nice try Scott, but I've already made my mind up and I can hear the police sirens now." He hung up.

The sirens in the distance became louder and Arnold forced the knife shaft into Robinson's already clasped hands through the chair's spell's, with the blade pointing upwards and outwards. He gripped Robinson's hands with his own, making the grip on the knife totally secure, ensuring his fingerprints were transmitted across to the wooden handle. He heard the police running up the path. It was time. He ripped tape from Robinson's mouth and with the knife held firmly in-between Robinson's hands and the end of the shaft supported upon a stool, the blade still pointing upwards, Arnold used his nineteen stone to fall heavily onto its point making certain that it penetrated around his heart area. He groaned as it deeply entered, and as the blood started oozing through his shirt, with a pen knife he quickly cut all Robinson's bonds before he fell to the ground, the carving knife still deeply embedded in his chest.

The police rushed into the room to find their colleague dying with Robinson stood over him.

A week later Scott was among many of Arnold's colleagues as they watched his body being lowered into the grave. The vicar said a prayer over him as D.S. Turner quietly spoke a few words to himself as he looked to the ground, a mixture of sorrow and guilt.

Jane Morgan could only shake her head unable to find words, always having looked up to D.C.I. Arnold.

"Is there any news on my mother?"

Scott turned to see Simon. "I'm so sorry. We've searched everywhere connected with Robinson and we won't stop until we find her."

Simon walked away in silence as Scott watched him. He shook his head. "What a psycho Robinson is" said Scott. "He's in a padded cell and apparently screams all through the day and night and keeps running at the wall, head butting it demanding the death penalty in different voices, different dialects. Fortunately, or unfortunately he wears a protective helmet."

Scott and his colleagues, after one last look at Arnold's grave, walked sadly away.

The end.

Printed in Great Britain
by Amazon